There

Get to know Verity Carmichael, Alexios Economides future bride! Inside their workplace relationship turned romance!

How could there be an inside look at something that didn't even exist? Verity felt nauseous.

Somehow, she was afraid that it was her fault. She could feel her control on everything around her beginning to dissolve, beginning to slip away. This job meant a lot to her. Pleasing Alex meant a lot to her.

She looked up, and she could see him striding toward her. She had the glass door of the office opened as soon as he approached it.

"I..." She winced. "Somehow, the media got a hold of the mistaken information that you and I are engaged."

He looked at her, his expression smooth. He didn't look surprised.

That tilted her entire world on its axis. She had been afraid of him being angry, but she hadn't imagined him being... Placid. Mostly because Alex was never placid. And he seemed suspiciously so right then.

"Oh? I did not intend for the press release to go out so quickly."

She blinked three times. "I'm sorry?"

"Yes. I gave the information to the media."

Millie Adams is the very dramatic pseudonym of *New York Times* bestselling author Maisey Yates. Happiest surrounded by yarn, her family and the small woodland creatures she calls pets, she lives in a small house on the edge of the woods, which allows her to escape in the way she loves best—in the pages of a book. She loves intense alpha heroes and the women who dare to go toe-to-toe with them.

Books by Millie Adams

Harlequin Presents

The Forbidden Bride He Stole
Her Impossible Boss's Baby
Italian's Christmas Acquisition
His Highness's Diamond Decree
After-Hours Heir
Dragos's Broken Vows

From Destitute to Diamonds

The Billionaire's Accidental Legacy
The Christmas the Greek Claimed Her

The Diamond Club

Greek's Forbidden Temptation

Work Wives to Billionaires' Wives

Billionaire's Bride Bargain

Visit the Author Profile page
at Harlequin.com for more titles.

PROMOTED TO BOSS'S WIFE

MILLIE ADAMS

Harlequin
PRESENTS

If you purchased this book without a cover you should be aware that this book is stolen property. It was reported as "unsold and destroyed" to the publisher, and neither the author nor the publisher has received any payment for this "stripped book."

Harlequin® PRESENTS™

ISBN-13: 978-1-335-21327-3

Promoted to Boss's Wife

Copyright © 2025 by Millie Adams

All rights reserved. No part of this book may be used or reproduced in any manner whatsoever without written permission.

Without limiting the author's and publisher's exclusive rights, any unauthorized use of this publication to train generative artificial intelligence (AI) technologies is expressly prohibited.

This is a work of fiction. Names, characters, places and incidents are either the product of the author's imagination or are used fictitiously. Any resemblance to actual persons, living or dead, businesses, companies, events or locales is entirely coincidental.

For questions and comments about the quality of this book, please contact us at CustomerService@Harlequin.com.

TM and ® are trademarks of Harlequin Enterprises ULC.

Harlequin Enterprises ULC
22 Adelaide St. West, 41st Floor
Toronto, Ontario M5H 4E3, Canada
www.Harlequin.com

Printed in Lithuania

PROMOTED TO BOSS'S WIFE

To Flo, for being the best

CHAPTER ONE

Verity Carmichael scrunched her brows together and gave her boss the grumpiest look she could manage.

"You aren't eating your salad," she said.

"I told you I didn't like salad."

Alexios Economides was one of the most feared and revered men in the tech industry, a dark imposing storm of a man who—at roughly six foot five—towered over everyone around him. His black hair was always swept back from his forehead, glossy like a raven's wing and with no indication he used styling products of any kind. It was as if every strand was held there through the sheer force of his will. His eyes were a deep brown, with one spot of red in the iris on the right one, she'd taken note.

Alex was unfriendly, ill-tempered, stubborn, maniacally controlled and as beautiful and sharp as a piece of cut obsidian. The blessing and many, many curses of Alexios Economides, et cetera et cetera.

Everyone was afraid of him.

Except Verity.

She hadn't been hired to be scared of him. She was his assistant, but more than that. He'd hired her to be his...

Conscience.

His Cricket, which she had pointed out once in reference to a classic cartoon, and he'd taken it on board as a nickname that she pretended to dislike, but secretly loved.

The idea made her smile just slightly as it always did, and then she frowned because she was trying to look grumpy.

"You did tell me you were going to try and eat more vegetables," she said. "So I decided we could have matching lunches today."

"Did I hire you to be my nutritionist?"

"No. You hired me to talk to you and to presumably listen to you also so when you said you wanted to eat more greens, I listened. I acted."

"Sneaky Cricket," he said.

She smiled. "I wasn't being sneaky. Eat your salad."

He seemed to not know what to do with the lettuce he stabbed up onto his fork.

"I wish I had a steak."

"Try wishing on a star, Alex, I hear your dreams might come true."

"What?"

"It's a... Never mind."

She'd worked for Alex for two years now and it was the weirdest, nicest job she'd ever had. Not just because she was thousands of miles away from her parents, her siblings and their assorted drama and living on the shores of the Aegean Sea. Not just.

That contributed to her happiness, though, without a doubt.

She liked this job because it was an interesting challenge. EconomicTech was on the forefront of hardware and software breakthroughs, with new, exciting innovations happening every few months. It was exciting to work in a company that was this dynamic. There was always a buzz in the building—unless Alex was walking through and then it hushed.

Verity could admit that maybe part of what she enjoyed was being the Alex Whisperer. That was what her coworkers called her. And she simply grinned in response.

That was another bonus of this job. She'd turned childhood trauma into a work skill.

She knew how to soothe; she knew how to smooth over every situation. How to sublimate her own feelings and show nothing but calm.

Blissful, cheerful calm.

She demonstrated her cheerful calm now by taking a smiling bite of her salad, which only seemed to aggravate Alex more.

It was odd to think this was her life now. All because one of her friends from college created an app for elite job postings where every employee would be prescreened, and prevetted. If celebrities could have their own dating apps, why couldn't major corporations and the rich and famous have their own job listings? With confidential terms, only visible by candidates who had agreed to keeping details to themselves.

Knowing the app creator was as vetted as it got, so even without a lot of job experience, Verity found herself approved and given access to the kinds of jobs most people could only dream of.

When she'd first seen the job listing, she had thought it odd. He wasn't only looking for an assistant; he was looking for a confidante. Someone to talk to him, not just about work, but about personal things. She'd been a bit nervous at first. Partly because he was an intimidating man (she'd googled him immediately when she'd seen the job listing) and partly because it seemed almost too good to be true.

Relocation to Greece? Great pay? Reasonable hours? Hot billionaire boss?

Even though there was a layer of protection provided by the system she'd used to get hired, she'd been secretly waiting to discover that "conversation" was code for Wear a Sexy Godzilla Costume and Stomp Around the Office to Satisfy My Dinosaur Fetish.

Which she'd said to him once, after she'd been working at the office for six months and he'd said, simply: "Godzilla isn't a dinosaur."

Then they'd debated what the best actual dinosaur was, because somehow that was her job.

He didn't want anything weird or sexual from her. He really *did* just want conversation.

She'd been given a small packet when she was hired that included a list of hard conversation limits, and she'd been happy to respect them initially because of the money and then later because she genuinely cared for Alex. How could she not?

That didn't mean she didn't wonder about him, of course.

She spent five days a week with him. When she wasn't with him, she thought about new topics she could cover with him. In a professional way, of course.

She didn't feel *like that* about him.

Sure, he was the most handsome man she'd ever seen. Probably because he was the most handsome man on the planet, in a purely aesthetic sense. But he was intense, and Verity could do intense from nine to five, but she would never ever ever sign up for intense in her personal life. In her home. In her heart.

No, thank you.

She was far more interested in men who were nice and smiley. In theory, since she'd never actually dated anyone at the very ripe age of twenty-four, which was starting to be bothersome. But Verity was nothing if not a problem solver.

She'd smoothly and cheerfully problem solved her way out of Oregon, away from her family, away from all the toxicity in her childhood home. She'd worked her way through college and gotten herself this job.

There hadn't been time to date.

There was now, though, and she had a lovely, *lovely* coworker named Stavros who was all the things she could want. He was close to her age, he looked lovely in his navy blue and tan suits that weren't anything like as severe as Alex's commitment to all-black everything.

She took another bite of her salad. "I think I'm going to ask Stavros on a date."

Alex's face did something she'd never seen it do before. It flashed between confusion, irritation and something else she couldn't pinpoint. Then it was like she could see him doing a math equation in his head, and get the answer in record time.

"Stavros from the accounting department who has worked for this company for six months?" he asked.

"That would be him," she said, demurely, crunching her lettuce.

"He is your superior, technically."

"We work in totally different departments and HR allows for romantic relationships at this company as long as both parties sign a waiver."

"I am aware."

"I assumed, but you were acting like maybe you didn't realize that."

"Of course I realize it, Cricket, but from a moral standpoint, he is your superior, and it is problematic."

It was so funny to hear those words come out of his mouth because she had a feeling he had no emotion behind any of them. What he had was a computer program he'd uploaded into his head to make sure he knew what was okay, and what wasn't.

Which was maybe mean, because he wasn't an unkind man—not really if you dug down deep and got to know him over salad—but he was...detached.

There was a reason she'd been hired to be his human connection.

He was deeply unpopular in a world that was skeptical of billionaires. Where investors wanted their money placed at ethical companies, and social media made memes out of every lip twitch and eyebrow lift.

And while the internet agreed that Alexios Economides was hot, in all the various forms the internet declared a man hot, from panting emoji to all caps declarations of DADDY beneath photos of him, they also agreed he was an evil, MORALLY GRAY billionaire who had ice in his veins.

The truth was, Alex was very ethical. He donated to a great many causes and he offset his carbon footprint judiciously. But it was the...general vibe of him. His good deeds couldn't transcend the fact that if he were to stand in front of a podium and tell the world that he was Hades incarnate, they'd believe him.

But that did make the lectures on morality ring a little hollow.

"Are you saying I don't have agency?" she asked, licking some dressing off of her thumb.

"Excuse me?"

"I'm a grown woman, and I like him. I want to date him and yes, he's in a more senior position than I am, I guess, in a department I don't work in, but I'm the one who wants to ask him out. Are you saying that my personhood evaporates when it comes into contact with corporate structure?"

"I'm not saying that at all."

"You kind of are. You're telling me that what I want is problematic."

"Men use positions of power to manipulate women."

"Thank you for that, Alex, I didn't know that until a

man in a position of power told me." She stared blandly at him and he shifted, a dark, unamused look in his eyes. Which amused *her* greatly.

He cleared his throat and her heart jumped in her chest, just a little bit.

"No one ever dares speak to me that way," he said, taking another angry bite of his salad.

"You hired me to talk to you like a human being and to teach you to talk to other people like a human being, and I have to tell you, you reciting a list of rules, divorced of context and emotion, doesn't really make you human. It makes you seem even more robotic."

She felt guilty as soon as that came out of her mouth because she could only assume that he'd hired an external conscience for social time in part because the commentary on him being AI rather than a human being made him feel bad.

She didn't want to make him feel bad.

Maybe that was a little bit silly, since most of the time Alex didn't care about making other people feel bad. Or rather, to be fair, he didn't *notice* when he did. Theoretically he was trying to learn—that was why she'd been hired. But often she wondered if she was making much of a difference beyond their lunches.

But he was... He wasn't like anyone she had ever known, and she had learned a lot from him. About technology and business, innovation. She...respected him.

She liked him.

Even when he was being ridiculous.

"I have a board meeting on Friday," he said.

He changed the subject so swiftly and abruptly it nearly gave her whiplash.

"About?"

"Attracting new investors ahead of the next product launch."

"I mean, it's a sensationally slick product. An AI assistant that uses less energy, and also learns from resources that actually gave consent is a really big deal. Not to mention it functions incredibly well."

"You really think the average consumer cares about the ethics of it?"

"Yes."

"They don't. They talk about it, they pretend to care and then they all pick their phones up like everyone else and never give a thought to how much energy is harvested to power that little square that lives in their pockets."

"You think all of humanity is hypocritical then?"

"I think at the intersection of convenience and ethics convenience often wins. But where I really do believe the product could succeed is that it is exceptionally convenient still. It's not the salability that concerns me, it's the fact that investors have been scarce in the past year, after that video went viral of me..."

"Breaking that kid's phone after he stuck it in your face?"

"He wasn't a kid, he was your age. And also, I clearly didn't break it well enough, because there's a video of the entire thing. From that point of view."

"Yes. It did not help humanize you." She paused.

"Though at least they called you the Terminator after that instead of Data."

It had been an uncharacteristic display of temper, though it had even had that same robotic, measured manner about it. He hadn't yelled or shouted. He'd simply taken the phone and thrown it to the ground while continuing on his way.

"I don't care what anyone thinks of me, but it's becoming a problem with investors. Which infuriates me." He said that with the same measured tone he'd been using the whole time.

She had to hold back a laugh. "I can see that. You're positively simmering with rage."

He had said all of it in the same calm voice. He didn't seem outraged in the least. Except for the burning embers in his dark eyes.

She knew him well enough to know that she needed to be somewhat careful when he got that look.

She had never seen Alex in a full temper, but she knew that the potential for it existed. And she was nothing if not an expert at avoiding explosions of temper, tamping them down and keeping them from ever occurring.

"At least the video proves that you're not AI," she pointed out. She had a feeling it was not the least bit helpful. And the irritated look that Alex gave her proved that theory.

"That was not a serious rumor," he said.

"It was," she said softly.

"So it's more believable that I was created in a data

mine by an advanced learning module than that I'm a rich man who prefers to keep to himself and stay away from social gatherings?"

"Well. I don't want you to get an inflated ego, but the thing is, you are young...sort of, and you're extremely good-looking. Obviously people expect that you would take the money that you've earned and spend it ostentatiously on parties and yachts. With yacht girls. Or yacht boys, if that's what you're into." She looked at him, and tried to see if there was any reaction to either proposed yacht person.

That was the strangest thing about Alex. In a world that made privacy next to impossible—with cell phones and algorithm-based social media taking small moments and putting them on a world stage on the daily, he remained relatively private. Unknowable. Except of course he had been caught being angry at an obnoxious moron, and somehow had been painted as the bad guy. Well, she knew how. He was the billionaire. The power differential was clear, et cetera et cetera. The expectation that somebody who had a public-facing persona—sort of—was a public commodity was one that Verity didn't agree with, but that didn't make it any less real.

"What do you mean *sort of* young?"

"Well, you *are* in your thirties."

He didn't quite scowl, but he was very close.

"I need you to come to the board meeting," he said.

"Of course I'll be there. It's my job."

"Yes," he said, in total and complete confirmation.

There was something so final and intense about it,

he might as well have been agreeing that he owned her in some capacity beyond work, because for some reason she felt like he had. Like there was something deeper than a work contract between them, when she knew there wasn't.

"I'm very helpful," Verity said, and she was teasing him, but part of her wanted him to agree. "I bet you feel better for having eaten a salad."

"I will feel better if I have a steak to follow it up."

"You're ridiculous. You don't need that much red meat midday."

He lifted a dark brow, and leaned back in his chair, which gave her full view of his rather muscular, perfectly hard torso. The crisp white shirt underneath his black jacket did not hide the structure of the musculature there; rather it turned into a sort of tease that appealed to her more than she wished it did.

She wrinkled her nose. "Are you trying to make a point?" she asked.

"Do you take a point by my posture? If so, then I suppose it is made."

"If you're trying to make the point that you having no body fat and well-defined muscles means that you don't need to watch what you eat, then you are woefully behind in regards to your education on health and nutrition."

"Which is another indication that I'm not AI."

"Why is that?"

"I would've been programmed with the latest data."

"More likely you would have eight fingers on one hand, but sure."

That actually did make him smile. It was never a full smile with teeth and crinkling eyes, nothing half so demonstrative with Alex. No. And so she took these rare, small flexes of the corners of his mouth as priceless gems. Because they were. And she had to remind herself yet again that their connection was boss and employee. That he wasn't really her friend. They never did anything outside of work, after all. They would be an improbable match in that regard.

She tried to imagine it. She thought of the things that she used to do at home with her friends. Imagined going through a drive-through coffee stand with Alex, and then going to the mall. It almost made her laugh out loud, but she held it back, because if she laughed, then she would have to explain herself to him.

"You are going to ask Stavros on a date," he said.

And yet again, his abrupt subject changes, which clearly came from some shift in his brain, invisible, sharp and beyond the understanding of everyone else, like all of his innovations, just about made her head spin.

"Yes."

"When?"

"I don't know. But I'm going to."

"You are going to wait and see if he's interested in you first?"

Verity scrunched her face. "No. Because I think that's outdated. I like him, so why play games?"

"I agree with you. It's only that I'm given to understand that games are an essential part of romance."

"Do you...often play games when it comes to romance?" She was skirting around the edges of off-limits topics. Well, actually this wasn't in the list of things they couldn't talk about; it had just always felt like she shouldn't talk about relationships with her boss. Also, it had never come up, since she'd never been in one, or even attempted to be until now.

Something flickered in his dark eyes, another near-imperceptible lift of his brow. "No. I don't. I don't have time for games. If I want sex I can have sex without romance."

Her face went very hot, and she wanted to go back and have never heard that word exit his mouth. She wanted to lecture him about boundaries. But this was the problem. They had personal conversations, she had brought up the subject of dating and she had asked him about his personal romantic life. The truth was, she worked for him, but two years of lunches put them in a space that was not entirely professional. No matter how much they should remain so.

"Spoken like an AI," she muttered, picking up her salad bowl and reaching out for his. He handed it to her without a second thought. Because yes, during lunch hour she was his...something. But after that she was an assistant. Of course genius hands like his did not wash dishes.

"Thank you for the salad," he said.

It was so shocking that it stopped her in her tracks.

She felt something like pleasure bloom at the center of her chest. "You're welcome," she said.

"Verity," he said, before she walked out, his use of her first name rather than the more common Cricket as shocking as the thanks.

"Yes?"

"The board meeting is in London. I've added some money to your expense account for new clothing, so why don't you spend the rest of the day preparing."

And while she should have spent the rest of the day planning how she might approach asking Stavros on a date, instead, as she browsed through the high-end shopping boutiques in Kolonaki, she heard Alex's *thank you* echoing in her head.

CHAPTER TWO

Alex watched his little personal assistant, who could never hide her abject fascination with his private plane no matter how hard she tried. She was always meandering around, opening drawers on furniture, looking inside the well-stocked bar, even though she barely ever drank anything stronger than a Shirley Temple.

She was a fascinating puzzle, was Verity. It was why he had hired her in spite of her lack of experience.

He had brought her in for an interview—a rare thing for him to interview an employee personally, but it was for the position of personal assistant, and more. Because he was beginning to recognize that his lack of human connection, his lack of personability, was becoming a liability.

Such a ridiculous thing.

He had power and money now. And yet still, he had to cater to the whims of others, especially ridiculous when those whims seemed to be created out of the air.

Created out of a false idea of who he was.

He wouldn't say he was a good man, acting out of the goodness of his heart, but he didn't do harm.

His life was his work. Which had made finding success possible in his early years. He had worked his way up in a small, inconsequential tech company where he had found a mentor in the owner. Eventually, he had taken over the business, then it had begun expanding, and he had renamed it. Had made it his own. And had turned it into something else entirely. A leading force in the tech industry, a global success.

Five years ago the company had become publicly traded, and then suddenly, the will of other people had been interjected into his success.

This was where conflict began.

Because it was no longer enough that he was brilliant, or that his product was superior. Small actions could affect the price of his stock, the willingness of investors could be swayed and shifted by public opinion, as everyone fought hard to play the cutthroat game of being beyond reproach in the eyes of a public hungry for that dopamine hit of moral superiority.

Which was why good deeds became public domain, charity was a public performance and attending galas, parties, places where a person could be seen being the sort of person others might be able to admire, was essential. And something that Alex had never personally seen the point of. Now he had to.

Or he could let it crumble. Could let his empire reduce itself, could go back to being a force in business, rather than the force. But relinquishing his grip on the gains he'd made simply wasn't something he was willing to do. And that was where Verity had initially come into the equation. He wanted to begin making moves to take his company to the next level. It had been suggested to him by one of his board members that he might try...practicing. That connection bit.

It wasn't that he didn't believe in it. It was just he had never had it. And therefore didn't especially understand.

He had been with child protective services from near the moment he was born. He didn't even know the circumstances around it. Why his mother had given him up, or why he had been taken away. Which thing it even was.

He had never—not from birth to the age of eighteen—been with a family for longer than six months. And where at first connection had merely felt foreign, it had become something he had guarded himself against. Because the end would always come. Because no one was attached to him, and so there was no point building an attachment to anyone else.

He'd honed so many skills that were valuable to him over the course of that childhood. Difficult though it was, it had made him into a successful man.

How horrendously ironic that the circumstances of that childhood should cause him to trip at the finish line.

No. He had not tripped; he had merely faltered. Now he had Verity, who everyone in the company loved. Verity, who made him eat salad and was currently poking around his plane like a nosy little mole looking for a hidey-hole.

"Sit down, Cricket," he said. "You're making me dizzy."

"I'll never get over how amazing this is. It's really more the house than it is a plane."

"No," he said. "It is a plane."

"You know what I mean. I think my apartment is smaller than this."

"Why?"

She looked at him, humor glittering in her eyes. She found him funny, which was a strange experience. He didn't think anyone else found him particularly amusing. "Have you looked at the prices for apartments in Athens these days? It's a bit prohibitive."

"I pay you very well."

She nodded. "You do. And I like to have money left over for savings, and to do things. I go to the beach almost every weekend."

"Do you?"

He had never thought about what Verity did in her spare time. Or where she lived. The idea of her doing things when she wasn't in his office was somewhat disconcerting, and he couldn't say why.

Of course, when she had mentioned asking Stavros on a date he had been forced to think of her in another context altogether, and he hadn't liked that either. She was…well, she was Verity. He didn't take much notice of other people. Their clothing, their likes, their dislikes, their moods. He'd hired her to teach him to engage with those things, to talk to him, and he found that he was highly tuned into all those things about her now.

She was going to sit and eat a meal with Stavros? Just as she did with him?

He found that uncomfortable.

"Yes," she said.

She turned from the bar, her gray plaid skirt swirling around with her, revealing a peek at her thighs. He didn't really want to look at his assistant's thighs, and generally speaking, if he didn't want to do something, he didn't. And yet.

She was a fascinating woman, though he would never say that out loud. He wasn't sure he had ever been fascinated by another person before. But she was just so different. From an entirely different world, a different life. While they didn't speak in depth about their families, or the lack of his, she had told him once that she had spent her entire childhood in the same house.

The idea had nestled in the middle of his brain, and centered itself on many afternoons when his mind had begun to wander.

What would it be like to grow up with that sort of stability? To not spend all of your life moving from house to house, between different neighborhoods in a city, or sometimes even hours away. All of your belongings wrapped up in black plastic, your lone pair of shoes on your feet, growing tight and worn, until someone finally noticed but you might need a new pair.

He had a room in his house dedicated to shoes now. He could wear a different pair every day. The moment his feet felt even the slightest discomfort, he would change the shoes.

It was his favorite luxury. That and knowing that he was in charge of where he slept every night. He had multiple homes, and if he wanted to move between them he could, and often he did feel a strange sort of burning sensation in his chest when he spent too many nights in a row in one place.

He had an apartment at the top floor of the office building, and the house up in the hills on the outside of the city. A place by the beach. He could offer to let Verity use it. He supposed.

Those were just his houses within proximity to the company's headquarters.

There were others.

It felt powerful to own so many pieces of the world, when he had owned nothing for so long.

And yet here he was, jumping through hoops he didn't care to even acknowledge.

Thus was the cost of success.

There was a point where one could become successful enough that they had to consider nothing and no one else, but now he had begun to arrive at a different part of the curve, where if he wished to continue to progress he had to care.

Verity sat on the love seat opposite him, a keen sort of expression on her face. "What is the meeting about?"

"The product launch."

"I understand that," she said. "But I mean what is the focus of this specific meeting? Why have they called it now, and what are you concerned about?"

"I didn't say that I was concerned," he said.

"No, you didn't."

He stared at her. "And?"

"I can tell you're concerned," she said.

How strange.

"My popularity is in question, as you know."

"Yes, I do know. But what are the real-world consequences to that?"

"A disappointing launch. And if we do not remain number one in the quarter during the launch period, then we will have ceded ground, and I refuse."

"Right." She leaned back, her blond curls fanning around her as she rested her head against the back of the love seat. Her hair was one of the first things he had noticed about her. It was wild, and she never tamed it. Even if it was up in a bun, she let tendrils fly free. There was something about that which captured his focus in a way he could not articulate.

It was, he thought then, something to do with the fact that it was so quintessentially Verity.

"But the question I have," she continued, "is what is enough? How many times do you need to be number one? Because success on this level surely can't continue forever. Everybody reaches a peak."

"That might be true when an entity is smaller than mine."

Her lips twitched. "An entity?"

He narrowed his gaze. "You know what I mean. Total domination is possible. And I want to."

"Why?"

How did he explain? How did he explain that in a world he had not asked to be born into, a world that had passed him around like a bad penny that no one wanted, he needed to make an undeniable, unquestionable place for himself? One that would endure after he died.

This launch was the one that would do it, and that made it more important than anything else he'd ever done. He had a chance to set a precedent with new technology, one that would carry on after he did.

He did not have a family. He never would, most likely.

The idea of love and marriage, of hearth and home, when he had never experienced it...

It was a blank space in his mind. He could not have conjured up an image of himself in it any more easily than he could fly.

Yes, he had seen it. Windows into it while watching TV, or worst of all, when he had been with good families in his years in foster care and he had sat down at dinner tables with parents who cared about their children, knowing that he would never be one of those children. Knowing that it wasn't a place that he would stay.

He would never hunger for something he could not have, not again.

This, this total dominion over his market, that he could achieve, and so he would.

He did not have to explain it to Verity, he decided.

She didn't need to understand. She simply needed to collect her paycheck.

He nearly said it to her, but didn't, because he needed her to look as sweet and rosy in the board meeting as she did right now.

"Because," he said. "Because I am an ambitious

man, and ambition only partly realized is nothing more than frustration."

"We don't want you to be frustrated."

She sat perched on the edge of the couch now, and he couldn't help but be amused by her London attire, gray wool and a check pattern which he had to admit was charming.

She was charming.

She had an effortlessness about her. A way of making others feel at ease. He didn't like to admit that she did the same thing to him that she did to everyone else. That she seemed to have some sort of magical ability to appease him, like he was a beast who needed soothing.

But she did.

He'd known she was the one he'd hire the moment she walked into his office, and it was like the tension bled from his muscles.

Verity was all things good. He had never thought that about another person before.

Least of all Stavros, who was quite competent in his position, or he wouldn't be working at the company, but he certainly didn't seem good enough for her.

He didn't say that either. Instead, he busied himself with work for the rest of the flight and when they touched down in London, he resumed watching Verity's reaction to everything.

"I would love to come back here on a holiday," she said wistfully as a town car swept them through the city streets, moving quickly to deliver them to the meeting.

"Then you will," he said.

He would give her a bonus. Whatever she needed.

That was another thing he had learned in the formation of this company. If you paid people well enough, they would always stay. His personality didn't seem to matter overmuch as long as they were well compensated.

He could pay people to stay with him.

That thought sat uncomfortably in the center of his chest.

He chose not to analyze it.

When they got out of the car, Verity paused near the entrance to a coffee shop, one that was next to the office building.

"What are you doing?" he asked.

"I think we should stop and get a box of sweets."

He was about to protest, or ask her why, but she was charging ahead, her phone held aloft in front of her, and he could see the digital version of the company's credit card gleaming on her screen.

She immediately charmed every employee in the place, and bought a box full of sweet treats—little cakes and scones and biscuits, which of course Verity called cookies. This did not seem to annoy the employees providing the baked goods; rather they seemed to find her effortlessly charming.

One of the workers behind the counter smiled at him, and he smiled back. The other person's smile faded, and Alex wished that he had a mirror to check his expression because he had been certain that he was being friendly.

Verity was now holding a pink box filled with sweets, and he held the door open for her as she rounded out of the shop, blond curls bouncing against her back.

"And what is this?"

"I'm going to put everybody in a good mood from the beginning. A little bit of cake never hurts, and neither does the gesture."

They walked into the building, where he was recognized on sight, and so they didn't have to stop at registration. Rather they simply stepped into the elevator. "But we don't even know if they're hungry."

"Of course not. But you don't have to be hungry to eat cake."

That was true.

"It's like any gift," she said. "It's the thought that counts."

They made the rest of the elevator ride in silence, and when the door swept open, Verity took the lead, and he watched her walk in the wrong direction, that pink box clutched tightly in her hands.

"Verity," he said. "This way."

She stopped and turned, and he tilted his head the other direction. Her cheeks went pink, and she scampered back toward him, and he took the lead, as it should be, the two of them headed into the meeting.

"Good morning," he said as he stepped in.

"Good morning," Verity said, the emphasis on the word somehow different, her voice wrapping around each syllable and making it seem warm. "I've brought some goodies to open things up. I'll get everything laid out while Alex… Mr. Economides…begins the introduction."

She set the box down in the center of the table and then left, presumably off to gather plates. Then Verity returned, and while he was speaking, she passed out plates and napkins. And took orders for coffee.

She turned the entire place into a café, and he found it irritating and distracting. Though none of the board members seemed to.

In fact, he had never spoken to such a charmed audience. It wasn't simply that they were interested in what he had to say, though they were, but they seemed… softer. More receptive.

Maybe it was cake.

Maybe it was Verity.

She went off to fetch a second round of coffee, at which one of the board members tapped him on the forearm. "She is delightful."

She was. She was delightful in a way he never could be. Never would be. In a way that seemed effortless.

She was relatable, to everyone somehow. She grounded the entire room. She was like a fairy, though he didn't believe in such things, and had never particularly been fond of childish stories. But there was something magic about her.

The mere fact of her being near him seemed to make everyone react differently to him, as well. The assumption being, of course, that such a sweet, caring woman would never associate with a man who was monstrous.

He could see it, and the way these people who he had met with many times before reacted to him now.

And that was just with her here as his assistant. How could he do this?

How could he bring what Verity offered him here out into the public eye?

Oh. He had an idea. More than an idea—it would happen. All he needed to do was set the wheels in motion. And it would be easy enough. It could coincide with the product launch. It was perfect.

He had hired Verity to be his personal assistant, and he had finally figured out what he needed her for most of all.

CHAPTER THREE

THE TRIP TO London had been all too brief, but Verity decided to turn her attention to Stavros, and her date goal.

She *did* think, a little bit, about the way that Alex had praised her after the meeting. He had told her what a good job she had done, and something had lit up inside of her.

Pleasing him was one of the nicest feelings she could think of. And it wasn't because he was more important than anyone else—it was only that he was so taciturn and difficult to read that when she knew he was happy with her it felt like something came alive inside of her.

She was used to walking on eggshells. She had grown up that way. In a house filled with volatile adults, who held everybody at the mercy of their moods. Her siblings had then learned how to weaponize those moods. Aim them at each other, and Verity had done everything she could to stay away from it. To stay away from them.

It wasn't like that with Alex. Yes, he had a mercurial nature. She could understand why people were afraid of him. But, she knew how to keep things running smoothly, and so she never took the brunt of his temper.

She didn't spend her time trying to avoid his ill will, and as a result, she was able to enjoy the feeling of earning his approval.

She collected those compliments; she thought of them as shiny rocks that she carried around in her pockets. Glimmering pieces of evidence that he was happy with her.

But, she wasn't going to think about Alex right now. Because she had chosen her outfit today specifically to ask Stavros on a date. She didn't usually dress sexy. Not that this was particularly sexy; it was just maybe a little bit bolder than her typical office fare. A purple dress that came a couple of inches above her knees, figure hugging and very flattering if she said so herself.

Her hair was especially wild today, but she had made her peace with her curls a long time ago. Once she'd stopped fighting them and learned to love them she had been much happier. And she had saved a lot of money on product.

Alex had texted her to say that he was coming in late today, which was all fine; she would see him at lunchtime. And then she could talk to him about how she had managed to get a date with Stavros.

She moved quickly down the hall, toward Stavros's office, her heart thundering in her chest. It was echoing just slightly in her ears. She had never done anything like this before. She imagined him, all sunny and pleased to see her, and that made her feel...

Not as good as pleasing Alex, but she wasn't going to dwell on that.

She paused at the door, and knocked.

"Come in."

She pushed the door open, and grinned when she saw him sitting there, just as she had imagined him. Dressed in his navy blue suit looking boyish and charming.

"Verity," he said.

His smile faded slightly, and Verity was confused.

"That's me. I wanted to talk to you."

"Really?"

"Yes. I... I was wondering if you...if you wanted to have dinner sometime. Maybe this weekend."

"Are you joking?"

"No. I'm not joking." Well, of all the responses that she might have received to her dinner invitation, that wasn't one that she had imagined.

"I just saw this."

He turned his computer screen so that it was facing her, and Verity looked at it as shock infiltrated her system. It was a photograph; that was the first thing that she noticed on the screen. A photograph of a London street, her in her little plaid suit, and Alex in all black as always, looking down at her as though he was giving an indulgent smile to a child.

And she couldn't even enjoy the fact that Alex had been caught on camera smiling at her, because her eye went to the headline next.

Tech Mogul Alexios Economides to Wed Personal Assistant!

She blinked.

"Is it true?" Stavros asked.

She didn't know what to say. She didn't know if Alex had seen this. She didn't know where the rumor had come from. She should just say no. It didn't matter what Alex thought, because this wasn't true, so there was no reason to let Stavros think that it was. The man that she wanted to go on a date with. Who she had just asked out on a date.

But if she said no, and... What if there was a reason? And it compromised her job? What if it made Alex angry, or it undermined something? As she stood there, trying to reason this truth quickly as possible, trying to figure out a way to extricate herself from the situation as peacefully as possible, she came to the conclusion that this must be some sort of mistake, but there was going to have to be a delicate extraction from the mistake.

Because it was public. *Grandly* public. This wasn't a gossip rag. This was being featured in a major journalistic publication.

And sure, they had gotten it wrong. Because of course it was possible for news sources to get things wrong. But she just needed to... She needed to talk to Alex. She took her phone out of her pocket and she started to text him.

"Is it true?" Stavros asked. She had totally blanked his existence for a moment. She looked up at him, and guilt gnawed at her. She realized that he looked hurt.

Maybe he did like her. She had to fix this. She just needed to...

"Please excuse me for a moment. I'm really sorry. This is... I just need to... Have to make a call."

She abandoned her text message, and opted to call Alex instead. He did not answer. She rang again, and again. He still didn't answer. What was going on?

She opened up social media, and she was shocked to see that his name was trending, along with hers.

She clicked on her name with a sense of growing hesitation.

Verity Carmichael.

There were so many posts.

Verity Carmichael is twenty-four and from Bend, Oregon. Get to know Alexios Economides's future bride!

Snag Verity Carmichael's look! Details here.

Is Verity Carmichael hiding a secret?

Inside the workplace relationship turned romance of Verity Carmichael and Alexios Economides!

How could there be an inside look at something that didn't even exist? She felt nauseous.

Somehow, she was afraid that it was her fault. She could see him storming into the office looking angry. She could feel her control on everything around her beginning to dissolve, beginning to slip away. Already, Stavros was mad at her, and maybe she shouldn't be worried about that right now, but she was. It made her feel queasy. Shaky.

This job meant a lot to her. Pleasing Alex meant a lot to her, and she was going to go ahead and admit that now as she stumbled toward his office. She sat there, a sheen of sweat beginning to form on her forehead.

Where was he?

She called two more times, and he didn't answer the phone. She knew that he had said that he was going to be in late, but it was strange that he wasn't answering the phone. Him being late did not mean that he wasn't working. Alex was almost always working.

And anyway, she was his…mistaken fiancée, so he should be in communication with her. Maybe he hadn't seen any of it yet.

She was going to have to break the news to him.

That made her palms get sweaty.

And then she looked up, through the glass walls that made up his office, and she could see him striding toward her. Could feel him, as if his energy transcended the barriers around her.

She stood up, and walked to the door. She had it opened as soon as he approached it. She started to speak, but words wouldn't come out of her mouth. Coherent sentences wouldn't form.

"I…" She winced. "Somehow, the media got ahold of the mistaken information that you and I are engaged, and it *very much* messed up my attempt at getting a date."

He looked at her, his expression smooth. He didn't look surprised. He didn't look upset.

That tilted her entire world on its axis. She had been afraid of him being angry, but she hadn't imagined him being...placid. Mostly because Alex was never placid. And he seemed suspiciously so right then.

"Oh?"

"It must be a mistake," she said.

"Must it?" He was serene, unruffled. It was...baffling.

"Yes, because we are *not* engaged."

"Indeed not. And I did not intend for the press release to go out so quickly."

She blinked three times. "I'm sorry?"

"Yes. I gave the information to the media."

Oh, so it wasn't baffling. He had gone behind her back and done the most insane thing possible that she would never have guessed in the entire world because *who would ever do such a thing?*

Your eccentric boss who pays you to eat lunch with him.

"You...you gave the information to the media. But we are not... We aren't... I told you that I was going to ask Stavros out."

She didn't know why she was coming back to that, except everything felt absurd at the moment, and returning to that one, grounding thing seemed as sane as anything else.

"Yes, I do remember you telling me that." She sputtered as he continued speaking. "And that is an unfortunate casualty of this turn of events. But I was thinking about it after the board meeting a few days ago, and I decided that the best, most beneficial thing for my image would be if you and I were to be married."

"That's.... Who in the world would think that was a logical thing to do? And what is this? 1950?"

"Do you think that culture isn't traditional anymore? Trust me, Cricket, they are. While the youths posture about their progressive ideals, they still very much gather information about someone's mortality and likeability from their romantic partnerships. And everyone loves you."

"I don't... You don't..."

She didn't even know what to say. She couldn't form sentences. She was standing at the center of his office flustered and speaking in half-realized, choppy sentences like a fool.

"This makes sense, Verity. I have an image problem and I need to fix it. This will work."

"And you didn't...you didn't ask *me*?"

She felt anger rising up inside of her, such an uncommon feeling, and one that she hated. She didn't do anger; she didn't do out-of-control. She was someone who kept her emotions in check at all times. This panic that was taking over her like a ravenous wolf was entirely unwelcome, and the howling anger that accompanied it was even worse.

She tried to calm herself down. Tried to draw a deep

breath. This was still Alex, and she still knew him. This was not something that she had expected from him, and indeed nothing that she had ever expected to deal with ever, but she was going to listen to him. Listen to his rational explanation. He was her boss, so she really did need to listen.

And, whatever he said, she needed to try and find a peaceful outcome to it. If she blew everything up she would lose her job; she wouldn't be able to stay in Greece because she wouldn't be able to afford it. Everybody knew that she was Alex's assistant, and now they thought she was his fiancée. So whether she liked it or not, she was in a pickle.

She needed to calm down, be a little bit mindful and figure out what the right thing to do was rather than responding in an emotional state.

Because she wasn't either of her parents, and she didn't fly off the handle at a moment's provocation.

"No. I confess I didn't think to speak to you about it. It is such a logical step."

"It's a logical step," she repeated.

"Yes. Everyone at the board meeting absolutely loved you. You humanize me. That's what I hired you for."

"You hired me to be your *assistant*, and teach you how to have...casual conversations."

"Yes. To humanize me. I realized that it would be much more effective to use you in that capacity in a public sphere."

"But you... You realize that this is my life. You are hijacking my life. This isn't nine-to-five, this isn't office work, you're talking about pretending to be engaged to me."

"Oh no, I'm not."

"Then I'm even more confused."

"I'm talking about *marrying* you."

She clenched her teeth together and had to breathe very deeply because if she didn't she was going to fall over. Or leap across the room and strangle him with his tie. "You must be joking."

He looked down, and then looked at her, like he was staring straight into her soul. "What do you want, Verity? I have spent two years having lunch with you, and I know who you like in this office, what foods you like to eat, your favorite recipes to cook at home. I know where you like to shop around Athens, and I know that you're from Oregon. I know what movies you like, and TV shows. We have talked about every casual, small thing under the sun. What I don't know is what you want to do with your life."

She didn't know why, but the question and the direct nature of his gaze made her teeth chatter. Made it hard for her to breathe, hard for her to think.

"I… I want to be independent. And to have enough money to support myself, but also enough time to enjoy where I live. I want to date. And make new friends, and go out and have fun. I want what most people in their twenties want."

"That's shallow," he said, waving a hand dismissively. "That's what everyone wants."

"I want to have enough that I never have to go back

to where I came from," she said, feeling raw and exposed by those words. Feeling goaded into saying them.

"And that is what I want. And it is also what I offer you. If you do this, if you marry me, for at least six months, and it has the desired effect, after which we will discuss the length and terms even more explicitly, then you and I will both achieve our goals. I will send you on your way with a very healthy hazard pay package."

She took one breath. Then another. And what he said began to sink in.

"What do you mean you'll send me on my way?"

"If this wedding and marriage are supposed to look authentic, then it would be very unusual for us to continue working together afterward."

Her head was spinning. He was proposing that they engage in a fake marriage, and that it would be the end of her relationship with him. Of course she had never imagined that this job would last forever. It had always been a weird job. From the moment that she had first agreed to it, it had seemed too good to be true, and definitely not something that would continue. In fact, she was somewhat surprised that she had been doing it for two years.

That he had continued to want to have lunch with her every weekday during that time.

But she was being torn in half by this. This thing he was proposing that she was still having trouble wrapping her head around. He wanted to marry her. And then he wanted her to go away.

But he was also offering her…

Independence.

"I don't want to get married," she said.

He hadn't asked, and she supposed it didn't really matter for the purposes of what he was talking about.

"I thought you liked Stavros?" he asked.

"I do. But I want to go out with him. And maybe..." The back of her throat felt prickly. "You know, I want the same things that you do when you go out with someone. I don't want forever."

Her cheeks heated. "No. I don't romanticize marriage."

How could she? Her house had been a war zone. She supposed she could be grateful that neither of her parents had abused each other or their children with their fists. But she had learned that psychological warfare could be just as damaging in many ways. It had taken her so long to rebuild any sense of value and herself.

The enormous weight she'd carried every day trying to keep the peace had left her exhausted. She'd put all her own emotions on the back burner to appease them. She had learned that she didn't matter, that everyone else mattered more.

In some ways, she felt like she had truly emerged from her cocoon after college. Those four years she had still felt like it might all be taken away from her at any moment. Like maybe she wasn't good enough or smart enough. Wouldn't be able to finish, wouldn't be able to amount to anything. She had also vowed to herself that she would rather be on the streets than ever go back home.

But because of that anxiety that had dogged her during her college years, she hadn't really had fun. She had been hoping to have some fun. And now Alex was asking her to pretend to be his wife.

Except…

She pressed her fingertips to her temples. "Wait a minute. There's a plot hole here. You think that I can marry you, and then we'll get divorced, and it won't just undo everything that we did with this relationship?"

She still wasn't entirely convinced that them getting married would do what he thought. Though, she could see what he was thinking. It would make him look like a man with an interior life, a man who loved someone, and had someone who loved him in return.

She didn't like the way that thought made her feel. It opened up a strange, yawning ache inside of her that she wished would go away.

And yet, even as she shoved that thought to the side, the feeling remained.

"I don't think that it will undo everything. Particularly not if we make it clear it ended amicably."

"It will just look like I signed an NDA."

"You will be doing just that."

"I already did," she pointed out.

"Yes. So you did. But I will have you sign another one. Because I will make it legally clear that I need you to keep my confidence personally as well as professionally."

Her heart was beating quickly again, and she tried

to calm herself. There was no way she was actually considering this.

"You knew that I was going to ask Stavros out," she said.

"Yes. And now I know he isn't the love of your life. Nor did you intend him to be."

Drat.

"But I like him. I wanted to..."

"You will not sleep with other men during the duration of our marriage."

You will not sleep with other men.

Those words scraped along her skin, down her spine; they froze her. Did he mean that she would...?

She stared at him.

Alex was a decade older than her, a billionaire. Hard, intense, everything that she had spent her life actively avoiding.

And here she was, embroiled with him in a way that she would never have been able to explain to younger Verity, who would not believe that she had gotten herself into this situation.

"Yes?" he asked.

Her brain was still frozen. She shook her head, and tried to catch her breath. "You don't mean...?"

"It will be a marriage in name only. We will make the terms of it very clear. You will perform the planning of the wedding. It will be available for public consumption. We will telegraph every part of this to a hungry public, and they will fall in love with you."

He looked at her, his dark eyes burning with conviction. She felt very much like she suddenly understood how it was to be Snow White, offered a poisoned apple. This was a poisoned apple, and she knew it. She still felt drawn to it. Still felt like she wanted it.

Like she might die if she didn't have it.

"You are special, Verity Carmichael. And the whole world will see it. What you did in that board meeting you will do writ large."

A small, angry part of her, wounded and curled up at the center of her chest, was so tempted. Her full name was out there in the media. Her family would see it. They would know that she had left home, and she had made something of herself. That the only reason she had ever seemed small or insignificant was because they had clipped her wings, and once she had some freedom, to heal, to find herself, she had found a way to fly.

If she married Alex, she would be married to one of the most famous, one of the wealthiest men in the world. She could help fix his company. It frightened her, how much that mattered. This idea that she could be responsible for fixing this. That she could be that important. She was the peacekeeper of her house, and she knew that it had been a toxic thing for her to have to do, but part of her still felt desperation where that was concerned. Still felt a deep, unending need to prove her worth. To make something better.

To show everyone that she wasn't the one who was broken.

And yes, it was going to cost her that date with Stavros, but Alex was right. She didn't hold out hope for love, not in the way most people thought of it. Yes, it would be nice. But the idea of living in some suburban fantasy, husband, wife, children, it made her feel almost nauseous. She had felt trapped in her childhood home, and she would be damned if she was ever trapped again. But this was different. This was different.

"I need to know your terms. Specifically."

He nodded. "I have had a document drawn up."

He reached into his jacket pocket, and took out a folded stack of papers. He thrust the sheaf into her hand, and she only looked at them. "I doubt it would be too much work for you to tell me what's in them. Considering that you're demanding I marry you, for real, put my life on hold and have this as part of my story forever, till the end of time."

He shrugged a shoulder. "It will be a marriage in name only. Of course I would never coerce you into intimacy. This is a business deal. Like I said, we will stay married for six months. With the option to extend the marriage by six more months if there is something critical occurring once the six months lapse. You will receive an allowance that is three times your current pay through the duration of the marriage. And then you will receive a lump sum upon the ending of the marriage. Which we will say ended amicably, in a united front. We will have a story that we both tell with matching details. Forever. No one is to ever know that the marriage wasn't real. Not your family, and if you do decide to marry at a later date, you may not tell him either."

Well, she wouldn't decide to get married later. And

she didn't have close friends right now that she would be lying to, and she wasn't going to invite her parents to the wedding. Later, when she did make the friends that she hoped to make, when she was traveling the world, which this would allow her to do, she might be sorry that she wouldn't be able to tell them the truth.

But wasn't that a small price to pay?

"I... How much is the lump sum?"

He tapped the paper.

She opened it slowly, and her heart leaped when she saw the amount written there. It was unfathomable. Millions of dollars. Enough to make her independently wealthy for the rest of her life. She could do...whatever she wanted. The only limit would be what she could imagine. For a woman who had always struggled with the concept of her own self-worth, that was a strange door to open up.

Money was a great reason to not follow your dreams.

But if she had all this money, she could. Which meant that she needed to figure out exactly what those dreams were.

But she would have the time to do that. She would have the time to make herself into a new person. One who wasn't so affected by her parents.

It almost felt like anything was possible. Anything would be possible.

She also knew that she could put up with anything. For a little while. Six months, maybe a year, with somebody that she already knew she liked spending time with. He wasn't asking for anything sexual. He wasn't asking her to give much of anything.

"What am I supposed to do when we are...married?"

"You will support me the way that you do now."

So she would still have her job. Which actually made her feel relieved. Because at least something would be normal.

"Then..." The truth was, she couldn't justify saying no to this. It would be criminally insane to turn him down. "Then I accept. Yes, Alex. I will marry you."

CHAPTER FOUR

HE HAD KNOWN that she would see his way of thinking. He felt immensely triumphant. She had come around to his way of thinking easily enough, and he had expected slightly more of a fight than she had given, if he were honest. But then, it was a good idea, and what he was offering her was generous. So what was there to argue about?

He decided that the wedding would be in one month's time, and when he sent that missive to Verity, she crashed through his office door not five minutes later.

"Yes, Cricket?"

If she had been a cat, he was quite certain that her fur would've stood up on end. "A *month*?"

"Yes. I don't see any point in dragging this out."

"You expect me to plan a wedding in a month?"

"I'm a billionaire, Cricket. If you need resources, you can buy them."

"I'm aware of that, but you know venues and…"

"We have to capitalize on the momentum of all of this. Have you seen the sheer volume of stories coming out just in the last couple of days?"

She stomped over to his desk. "Of course I have. They're impossible to ignore. Everyone is obsessed with you being in love. This is the most PR you've ever gotten, good or bad. It's...overwhelming."

"Perhaps for you. But I've never cared what people said about me."

She blinked, then huffed. "Then why are you doing all of this?"

"I don't care what other people think about me, but the board does. Investors do. That's my problem. This is all strictly business, and none of it's personal to me."

"Has anything ever been personal to you?" He had the feeling that it was a loaded question, but he didn't really know why it would be. He didn't know why she would care.

"I enjoy our lunches," he said, because he had the feeling that was what she was getting at.

"But not so much that you think of me as a whole person. Because you wouldn't just announce the engagement between yourself and someone who was equal to you without checking with them."

"Why do you think that?"

"Because that's not what people do."

"That's what I do," he said. "And I'm the same no matter who I'm dealing with."

She was silent for a moment. Then she sat down in the chair just in front of his desk, a blond curl falling down at her face, and he felt the urge to brush it away, though he didn't do it. Because he didn't cross that boundary with her. Ever. Of course, it would be a necessity, to an extent. When they were seen out in public together, they would have to touch.

The very idea of it made a strange, unwanted sort of heat unwind itself in his stomach, made him feel like he was at the mercy of something. And he didn't do helpless. Not these days.

So he pushed it down. Ignored it. Pushed forward.

"That isn't really true," Verity said softly. "You have always been nicer to me. I suppose that's why I thought maybe you would treat me differently than you do the other people around you."

"How do you think I treat the people around me?"

"Like pawns on a chessboard. Like conveniences or inconveniences, but not really like people, and I thought that there was something more to you, Alex, I really did. After two years of taking lunch with you every day, of talking to you about the weather and TV, and...life. I thought that we were friends."

The word sat uncomfortably in his chest, like a brick, and he couldn't grasp why that would be. He had never thought of Verity as a friend, but then, he had never thought of anybody as a friend. But maybe she was right. The way that they had interacted was perhaps something like friendship. And yet, he was still... He still felt as if there was a wall between himself and her. As there was with him and everyone.

A necessity as a child who was never allowed to have attachments, and a matter of course as a man who had never learned any other way.

"I don't have friends," he said.

He regretted it the moment the words left his mouth, because she looked wounded. Like he had slapped her, rather than simply speaking a simple four-word truth.

"It isn't personal," he said. "I don't know how to have friends. I don't have family. I never have. I assume you know I was raised in foster care—that much is public knowledge on the open internet."

She nodded slowly. "Yes. I do know that. But I'm not allowed to ask you about it, it's in my folder."

"Then I will tell you," he said. "I never stayed in one home longer than six months. I have never understood the attachment that people have to one another. Because there has never been anything remotely permanent in my life, nor has there ever been an expectation of it. I never knew my parents. I never will. I don't know why my mother gave me up, I don't know why my father wasn't involved. There is a great, dark void there, and it's one I stopped looking into a long time ago. I'm not sad about it. But it is what made me. That's why we were having lunch together."

"I thought I was sort of...coaching you or...?"

"It was just to get some idea of what it might be like. Of why people do it. How to look like I do it. Whatever I needed to do to bolster the sales of the company."

"So none of it was actually for you? None of it has been to try and...fix...?"

"I'm not going to be *fixed*. Handily, I'm not broken. You cannot miss what you've never had, little Cricket. I don't miss my mother because I didn't know her. I don't miss my father because I've never had one. I created this company and it has been my life. It is what gives me purpose. It's why I wake up in the morning. It is, I suppose, the one connection that I have truly on this entire planet, and I will do whatever I must to make it all that it can be."

She looked stunned. He had never told anyone all of this before, because why would he? It wasn't anyone else's business, and he didn't like the pity that he could see in her eyes. He didn't need pity. He was successful. He was a man who had overcome. A man who had transcended his circumstances, and he didn't need pity from anyone.

And here was this little thing looking at him as if he was a wounded animal. She didn't speak, though. That made him even angrier, because she always had something to say, and the fact that she was being careful spoke to the depth of how much she felt sorry for him.

No one was connected to him enough to feel sorry for him. He didn't want it. And it was unearned.

"Don't look at me like that," he said. "I am still your boss."

"My fiancé," she said softly.

"Employed to be my fiancée," he said. "And so I'm still your boss."

"And not my friend."

"I'm sorry if that hurts you. It's got nothing to do with you."

"Of course not. Why would it? There's nothing personal about any of this, is there?" She stared at the wall behind him, her expression as angry as he'd ever seen it. "Why did you choose me?"

There were reasons. But it was hard to take the shape of those reasons, those feelings, and put them into words. He knew them, but he didn't know how to lay them out to her. And so, he didn't. "You were the first person I interviewed."

The unspoken truth was that he was impatient, overly efficient, at the cost of anything else.

His words made her shrink.

But maybe that wasn't a bad thing. He needed to establish the boundaries here. Because while he was pleased that she had agreed to his plan, he could see that this might become difficult for her. Marriage meant nothing to him. It was as theoretical as all other connections, those mystical bonds he couldn't access, and didn't want to anyway.

She claimed she didn't plan on getting married but she was twenty-four years old, and the truth was, he didn't believe her. She didn't think she wanted to get married, but most people around him seemed to want it, seemed to fall for it in the end, as feelings of loneliness and inadequacy, and swiftly passing time overtook them.

She might think she felt that way now, but he doubted she would feel that way always.

"Well, I suppose that answers that question." Something in her demeanor shifted, there was a sort of distance that came over her and she straightened her shoulders. "If we only have thirty days then we need to begin making appointments. I feel like you and I need to be seen together. There needs to be ample media fodder, because if we're going to do this then we need to do it right. I'm going to need a ring, a dress and various other bridal accessories. We need a venue, flowers, music. Food. A guest list."

"Normally I would put you in charge of several of those things, but you're correct. We need to do the forward-facing work as much as possible. I will have someone in administration handle the venue, music, food and the guest list."

"Acceptable. I will find the best places for you and I to shop for some of these other things together. And I will present you with a modified schedule."

"A modified schedule?"

She nodded. "Yes. This is your priority now. It has to be. That's simply the only way this is going to work."

"I find that to be extremely heavy-handed of you."

She stood up, and she shot him a narrow glance. "*Do* you? What's good for the Cricket is good for the devil, ponder that."

And then she swept out of his office without a backward glance, and he would never admit it to her, but he did ponder that.

CHAPTER FIVE

VERITY HAD BEEN concerned that she overplayed her hand in Alex's office the other day, but he had acted like he wasn't offended by her during all of their following interactions.

She hated to admit that he had hurt her feelings. She didn't want to unpack any of that. She didn't want to examine it too closely. He was her boss. Her boss that she had agreed to enter into a sham marriage with, so there was a lot there.

And when he had looked at her with those dark, fathomless eyes and said that he had chosen her simply because she was the first person he had interviewed? It had been like a dagger to the heart.

So had what he'd said about his experience in foster care.

No one had kept him for longer than six months? For his entire life?

She was forced to imagine him as a little pinball, being bounced around the system with nowhere to rest. And then she supposed at eighteen he had been out on his own without a support system. There was no way that wouldn't have shaped who he was. It made her understand him to an extent. And made her worry a little bit that he was right. That he wasn't ever going to be able to have human connection the way that other people did.

She had read about things like that. That children needed to form bonds with caregivers before the age of two or they were damaged irreparably.

That just didn't seem fair, though. He hadn't had control over any of that.

It mitigated some of the anger she felt toward him. But just some of it.

It was weird, not having the specter of her Stavros crush standing between her and Alex. She didn't want to ponder why that was different either.

Stavros.

She scrunched her face. She was supposed to be meeting Alex in twenty minutes to go to a jewelry store, and it just occurred to her that she had never followed up with Stavros the previous week. She did feel like she owed him an explanation. But now she was going to have to come up with a lie.

She let out a heavy breath, and slipped down the hallway, finding his office door slightly ajar. She wrapped her fingers around the edge of the door, and pushed it open slowly. "Hi," she said.

He looked up from his desk, and for some reason, she just didn't get the same thrill when his eyes met hers. Eyes that were black like a void. She probably should have found a new therapist when she moved to

Greece. It was a little bit too late to worry about that, she supposed.

"I didn't expect to see you," he said.

"I'm sorry. I feel like I owe you an apology. There was obviously a bit of a misunderstanding between us. I haven't been in Greece all that long… You know, comparatively. And I really enjoy talking to you. And I thought that maybe we could be friends. But I realize that the way that I asked you to spend time outside of work might have been misinterpreted, and it had some very strange timing."

He frowned. "I see."

"I'm sorry. I imagine women generally don't just want to be friends with you."

He laughed, and leaned back in his chair. "That makes me sound like a jerk," he said.

"Well. No. It doesn't. It's just…" She felt like a jerk. Because she was the one who was lying to the man. Gaslighting him, really. But she was trying to do it in a nice way. "I can see in hindsight how it looked. And of course Alex was very protective of the nature of our relationship because he is my boss, and he actually takes all the appropriateness of all that very seriously."

"Does he? Because it seems to me like you were in a pretty easy position for him to take advantage of you, speaking of the fact that you are only newly in this country and you do work for him. Plus, you're quite a bit younger than he is."

"I do have agency," she said, using the exact same line of attack against Stavros as she had on Alex.

"I didn't mean to say you didn't. Only that there is definitely an appearance of impropriety," Stavros said.

"Well, there wasn't. But that is why we were so careful. We both understand how it looks. Anyway, I just wanted to clarify, because I feel like I looked really flaky, and maybe even not very nice, and I didn't want to hurt your feelings and..." Suddenly, Stavros was looking behind her, and he went a shade or two paler.

She turned, and there he was. Dark eyes like a void. Radiating dark flame.

"Verity. We were meant to meet."

Verity snatched her phone out of her bag, and looked at the time on the screen. "Not for ten more minutes."

"I expect to be able to find you in your office."

"I don't live in my office, Alex."

A muscle in his jaw jumped, and she could see that he was legitimately angry. She needed to get this out of Stavros's office before something blew up. She didn't know what, and she didn't know why, but she knew that something was in danger of exploding.

"Thank you," she said to Stavros. Which was maybe the wrong thing to say? But she was in a hurry. "I'll... see you later." Then when she reached out and grabbed hold of Alex's arm without thinking, and began to drag him away from the room, she was completely engulfed by him. His hardness, his heat, the overwhelming sensation of what it was to touch him.

She lost the ability to think, the ability to speak. He smelled like Cyprus. Like the sea. She wanted to lean in and smell him, sniff his jacket, right where it fell against his bicep. She wanted to move her hand up from where she gripped him at the crook of his elbow and touch that bicep.

Oh dear. She was drowning. In her embarrassment at having all of this happen in front of Stavros, in her anger at Alex for being... Alex, and in this new hell of knowing that touching him turned her into a creature made entirely of sensation and need.

And this is why not having the illusion of Stavros is a problem...

She wanted to strangle that sage inner voice.

"What was that?" she asked, letting go of his arm and turning toward him as soon as they were out of view of Stavros's office.

"Not here," he said.

He took hold of her again, and practically frog-marched her to the elevator, and as soon as they were closed inside, he released his hold on her. "I don't need you causing gossip by speaking to another man that you formerly had feelings for."

"That I formerly had feelings for? How do you know I don't currently have feelings for him? This is not real," she said, gesturing wildly between them.

"I didn't mean in reality," he said. "I mean it was terribly obvious to anyone who looked at you that you had a crush on him."

"Oh, I know. Which is why I was in there trying to come up with a different story for him, because he is very confused as to why I asked him on a date, only to have a headline about our engagement come out that very same day."

"Right," said Alex, clearly having only just thought of this for the first time. Because of course that would mean thinking outside of himself more than he was accustomed to doing.

"Yes, right. He is in fact the reason I knew that we were engaged, because you didn't tell me. So I had to explain...all of that, or we were going to have a loose end. And then you came in there like...like that, which only made things look weird."

"Aren't men often jealous when their fiancées speak to other men?"

"Insecure men, maybe."

He said nothing, and a muscle jumped in his jaw. He was actually upset. He was unhappy that she had been in there talking to Stavros. He couldn't be jealous, it was... He was possessive. In the way he might be of a paperweight that he really liked. Because they weren't friends, but there was a strange sort of...something. He tried to deny it, he tried to play it off, but it was there. He might not understand connections between people, but she did. She was very sensitive to them, and she maybe understood them a little bit better than she even wanted to. Because the kind of life she'd had growing up had forced her to be so very aware of the inner workings of people around her at all times.

It wasn't her that was wrong about the two of them. It was definitely him. But she did understand now that it wasn't…it wasn't quite a typical sort of connection. Because he didn't understand those sorts of things.

The elevator arrived at its destination, and they walked out the doors in unison. Then they stood there, side by side in the lobby of the building. "Hold my hand," he said, looking at her, his dark eyes presenting something like a challenge.

She took a deep breath, and curled her fingers around his. She was shocked by how rough his hands were. He was a man with a desk job; she didn't expect to find calluses there. His hand was so big. It overtook hers entirely. Just as he would if he were to…take her into his arms, press her against the wall…

She needed to stop thinking like this.

He was beautiful, and she had known that from the first day she had met him, but it had been easy to put him in his own category. She had made a lot of decisions about what she wanted her life to look like when she had left home. And one of the first decisions she made was regarding romantic relationships.

She didn't want someone volatile. She had felt like it was important to make those decisions before she had ever jumped into the dating pool because she knew that romance could make people silly. Alex had not been a viable candidate for romance of any kind, not just because of his age, or because he was her boss, but because he exhibited the kinds of characteristics she wanted to stay away from.

Friendship was fine. Even though they weren't friends. Her being his employee was fine, because she actually was so good at managing intensity that it was second nature to deal with him. But...

There was a very good reason that any attraction she felt had needed to be squashed instantly.

She didn't want anything to do with...that feeling that he created at the center of her chest. It was like there was a tuning fork just there at the center of her rib cage, and looking at him struck it, sending a note radiating throughout her entire being. It had been that way from the first moment she set eyes on him, and it had been her cue to find something else to distract her. Someone else.

And now she was holding his hand.

Grappling with the intense honesty unraveling inside of her. Because she hadn't thought all of this through. It was her natural instinct. Her survival mechanism kicking in. She hadn't thought: *Do not ever look at this man, look at this one instead who will never create complicated emotions inside of you, but will feel easy and fun. No, really don't look at your boss, because he could wreck you.*

It had been as natural as a gazelle turning and running from a predator in the grass.

But now that her skin was touching his she was forced to engage with the truth.

This was dangerous. She had walked straight into the lion's den.

Or maybe more appropriately she had taken herself right down into the underworld, into Hades's lair.

It was difficult to feel any sympathy for Persephone when she caused her own problems.

"Are we taking a car?"

She shook her head. "No. The jewelry store's just several blocks up that way, and I thought it would be good if we walked. Because you know..." She cleared her throat and started to walk. He was behind her a step for only a moment, and then took the lead, which she thought was absurd, because he didn't even really know where they were going.

"I'm the one who knows where it is," she pointed out.

"You said this way. I'll find it."

For some reason that felt poignant to her. She should be mad at him. Instead, it made her think about his childhood. About how he hadn't had anyone to guide him all that time. Of course he'd had to be decisive. Of course he'd had to take the lead even when he didn't know where he was going.

And look where it had gotten him.

Why are you feeling sympathy for him when you should punch him?

The paradox of Alexios Economides. The rest of the world might look at him and see an emotionless man with all the power and money in the world who didn't deserve any sort of compassion or sympathy or leeway. She saw something else, and she hated that she did.

Because had she done enough human projects in her life? She knew the outcome of it too. Nothing she had ever said or done had changed the way that her parents acted. And her siblings had followed right along with them. They had no self-awareness; they had no desire to be better, to be different. It was like everybody was born into the same toxic sludge and decided to keep rolling around in it. It could never be her.

It could just never be her.

But she didn't see toxic sludge when she looked at Alex, unfortunately. And part of her did want to change him.

She was relieved when they came upon the jewelry store, because it gave her an excuse to talk, and not think anymore. And definitely not focus on the way it felt for her hand to be in his.

When they walked into the glorious store, they were greeted by a short woman with a blunt bob and bangs, and glasses that took up over a third of her face.

"Good afternoon Mr. Economides, and bride," she said. "When I received the notification that you wished to come in and have a look at the jewelry selection today I immediately cleared the schedule."

Alex regarded the woman coolly. "How lovely. Though, it was my bride, Verity Carmichael, who made the arrangements for today."

There was a subtle scolding in the words, as though he was making it clear that she was to be addressed as an equal to him. The problem was, it was performative. Funny, because she had never really seen Alex perform. Normally, he was exactly who he appeared to be.

She didn't think she liked this.

Because there was always a little bit of distance between the two of them. There was distance between

Alex and everyone. But this was different. This required translation. She wasn't used to having to do that with Alex.

"Apologies," the woman said. "Of course. My name is Laura Braxton, and I'm the manager of the gallery. Whatever you're looking for, we have it here."

She looked at Alex. "I... I don't know what I want," she said. That much was honest.

"I know exactly what you should have," Alex said.

"Oh?"

He nodded. "I would like to see a selection of pink diamonds. Yellow gold for the setting."

Perhaps Alex had never been engaged before but she wondered how many women he had bought jewelry for. But then, as he had said only recently, he didn't need romance to get sex. She had certainly never seen him buying jewelry for anyone before, and yet he seemed utterly at ease and confident in this setting.

Though, that was just him.

He seemed to take for granted that he belonged wherever he was.

The trick she had never mastered. She always wanted to make herself small. Make herself disappear so that she wouldn't be visible, so that she wouldn't cause any problems. And wouldn't have any anger directed at her.

She had learned not to do that, but it still wasn't second nature to stand like he did, with straight posture and broad shoulders, like he was the master of all he surveyed.

Ironic, because it seemed like the world was asking

him to show a little bit more humility. Normally, she would enjoy that on a poetic level, because so many times in life men were given passes that women simply weren't, but in this instance, she found it annoying.

Because Alex wasn't the standard rich boogeyman that needed to be taken down. He had been through... hell. He had clawed his way up into his position. He hadn't been handed something by a dying relative, given chances simply because of who he was related to. She thought that should matter. That people should see who he actually was. Instead, they wanted him to sublimate his trauma and perform for them in the way they saw fit.

Honestly, she would be really annoyed about it if he hadn't just co-opted her entire life.

It only took a moment for a tray of pink diamonds to appear.

Verity had never given much thought to what sort of ring she would like.

Mainly because she had never thought about getting engaged. Of course, if she wanted a ring she could buy one for herself, but nothing this beautiful.

How had he been *right*? That was what she couldn't understand. Because these were the most beautiful rings she had ever seen in her life. Gleaming pink surrounded by that glorious gold. There was one at the center, pear shaped surrounded by darker pink gems in the shape of seeds.

"You found one you like," he said, his eyes trained on her, not on the jewels. She felt like she was pinned to the spot. Felt like he was looking into her, and it wasn't the first time she had felt that with him.

She didn't know how he could maintain that he was entirely unable to connect with people, that he didn't know a way to make them...like him, when it was so clear to her that if he took a moment he could see exactly what another person was thinking. He was insightful. Not just with machines.

Maybe it was just it was a skill he had never valued before, so it wasn't one he overly identified with.

One he didn't care about.

"Maybe," she said.

She was very aware that they were supposed to seem like a normal couple. That she needed to appear to be flirting with him, or something. But she was as much a novice at that as he claimed to be. The only man she had ever tried to flirt with was Stavros, and that hadn't gone well at all. Of course, that was Alex's fault.

He reached his hand out, and he plucked the exact one she had been looking at from the center of the tray. "This one would suit you," he said.

She didn't want to betray how beautiful she thought it was. That he had chosen the one she had set her sights on unerringly. But she didn't know how to hide it either. This was such a strange moment, outside of his office, unguarded without the strictures of their work environment.

In the office, they had a set pattern for how to be. But out here, they had held hands. And now he was standing there holding a ring out to her. She could only think to do one thing in response. She extended her left hand, and tried to ignore that her fingers were trembling. She knew that he would be able to see it. She knew that she couldn't hide this.

He said nothing, though; he merely extended his own hand, and took hold of hers. Then with his other slipped the ring onto her finger. It fit perfectly, like she was some sort of corporate Cinderella who was most definitely going to turn into a pumpkin at midnight—or at least six months from now.

But it was perfect. Beautiful beyond measure, and when she looked up into his eyes her breath was pulled straight from her lungs. She couldn't move. It was something like being prey in the sights of a predator, and yet it felt all the more dangerous. There was a sickly sweet feeling in the back of her throat, and her limbs felt languid. There was a deep response at the center of her thighs that she could feel yawn through her entire being. These were feelings she had never experienced when she had looked at Stavros. She had felt something pleasant when she interacted with him. Butterflies.

This was nothing like that. It wasn't the fluttery feeling you got with a grade-school crush.

This was decidedly adult, and was something she hadn't been looking for. But it had come and found her all the same. Perhaps that was why she felt hunted. And he was still touching her, his hands hot and rough, still looking at her, those eyes fathomlessly deep and utterly unreadable. If he was feeling what she did, she would never know. His was the black unknown of the darkest sea.

"Yes," he said. "This will be perfect."

She took a breath, desperate to gain her footing back. To gain some of her own back. He might be her boss, he might be older, he might be more experienced in life, in the world, but they had sat across from each other eating lunch for two years, and she would be damned if she let him make her feel small.

"I need to look at rings for him as well." She smiled at the attendant.

"Of course."

"Gold," she said. "Yellow gold. I would prefer something with symbolism."

"It will only be one moment."

He didn't say anything, but he was watchful in that way of his. That way that let her know she might well be in danger. That was just fine with her.

She would take the danger. She would take the challenge.

A tray was presented only a few moments later. Rings of gold, many woven together in a knot pattern. But her eye was caught by a simple design, a gold band with a geometric pattern that she recognized as being quintessentially Greek.

"What is that?"

"Oh," the woman said, picking up one of the gleaming rings and holding it out toward her. "This is Meandros. The interlocking pattern is unbroken and is a symbol of infinity."

She was suddenly filled with spite. And took the ring out of the woman's hand, and held it in her palm. "I think that will be perfect. Unbroken. Eternity. With the one thing you value most." She lifted her eyes and met his gaze. Of course anyone watching would think that she meant her. What she meant was his company. This would be her wedding gift to him. She would pay for it herself out of her outrageous earnings. Because the one thing he would have left would be his company. She needed to remember that. That this had nothing to do with her. That there was nothing romantic about it.

Of course he had managed to choose a ring that was perfect for her. Because he knew her. Perhaps that was why it had been so easy for him to manipulate her into doing this.

You were hardly manipulated.

She wanted to snuff her inner voice out like a misbehaving candle. She hadn't asked for a fair and balanced reporting of the situation. She wanted to feel sorry for herself. Standing there wearing a diamond ring with astronomical value.

"If that is what you think suits us best, my Cricket," he said.

"I think so. But unfortunately you can't wear it until the wedding."

"Unfortunately," he said.

He selected a matching band to go with her ring, and those jewels were packed up and sent back to his home, while she wore the outrageous engagement ring on her hand.

From there they went to the bridal store, where he sat in a room by himself while she tried on gorgeous bespoke gowns made of the most glorious fabric she had ever beheld. Buttery smooth and light. This wasn't a real wedding, but she didn't plan on ever getting married. So she let herself get lost in the fantasy. There was no other man she ever meant to do this with.

She put on a strapless gown with a sweetheart neckline with a glorious chiffon overlay that made her look like she was floating when she walked. The trouble was it was far too easy to imagine walking toward Alex like it was something romantic. She felt dizzy after the whole day. Everything was Alex, everything.

That moment in the ring shop.

She had tried to gain her own footing back. But...

This was all beginning to get to her.

When she was out of the gown and back in her street clothes, Alex came back and pointed at a vivid pink dress on a mannequin. "And what is that?"

"A special occasion dress." The attendant looked at him. "Would you like me to get that down for her to try on?"

"Yes. She can wear it to dinner."

Verity didn't have time to argue before she was bundled back into the dressing room, and practically stitched into the dress. It had a flowing skirt, and the top gave away almost every secret she possessed.

The attendant gave her a pair of hot pink Barbie heels to put on with it, and when she stumbled out of the dressing room like a frightened, sexed-up baby deer, she was sure that she must look ridiculous. She didn't look at the mirror. Rather she looked at Alex's face. And she saw...

Exactly what she had hoped to see when she had played games with his wedding band. He was the one who was dumbfounded. Except she realized, it wasn't about a ring, or about her knowing him. It was her boobs. Which was actually not all that satisfying.

Liar.

Okay. Maybe it was a little bit satisfying to know that she had affected him in some way.

"Perfect," he said.

She was hungry for more. For something. For it to not feel like there was a wall between the two of them. She wondered if she was asking for just a bit too much. But the way that he had looked at her had hooked on to something inside of her, was forcing her to reckon with some hard truths.

If she didn't have Stavros to distract her then she had to admit that she found her boss more compelling than any other man she had ever met. Her boss, who was absolutely, unequivocally the last man she should ever be interested in.

Not only because he was her boss, but because he was everything she had ever told herself she needed to avoid. He could hurt her.

She had been hurt enough.

So she locked down any of the feelings that were trying to claw their way to the surface, and she met his gaze. "Perfect for?"

"Dinner. We are dining in the city tonight."

CHAPTER SIX

THE AMOUNT OF money he paid for the garments that she bought, shoes, undergarments, the dresses, was enough to make her eyes bleed, and when they arrived at the restaurant in question, she was still reeling.

The restaurant was beautiful, with climbing vines all down the side. Those same climbing vines continued onto the rooftop, a canopy of green raining down over the diners. A glorious balcony with vine-covered walls, and a view of the Parthenon stretching out before them.

All heads turned to look at them when they walked through the dining area, and she had to wonder if it was because of just how chesty her dress was. Though, then she rationalized that Alex was very famous. And of course it had to do with the fascination of him, and definitely not her rather average rack. The truth was, it was only unusual to her that she was showing this much skin. It wasn't notable to anyone else.

Except maybe Alex.

But then, he also knew her. So he knew that this wasn't typical for her.

Maybe she should've pushed back when he suggested

the dress, but part of her felt lovely in it. So it was convenient to hand over the decision to wear it to Alex, rather than having to own it herself.

Was she that big of a coward? She asked herself that as they were seated in the most glorious spot on the rooftop, the warm breeze fluttering through her hair, the view of all that ancient glory giving her goose bumps.

It wasn't because of Alex.

"This is what you wanted?" he asked.

"We definitely have left an impression all over the city today," she said. She had considered, for a split second, acting like she didn't know what he was talking about, but there was no point. He was only thinking of the game. And all of the conflicted feelings that she'd had over the last few hours were only hers.

She needed to remember that. That no matter how tempted she was to think there was some sort of personal connection between the two of them, there wasn't. No matter how much she liked to scratch at him and mention her agency, he did have power over her.

Yes, she was getting something in this bargain, but she was only agreeing to it because it opened up avenues for her. If she were independently wealthy, then she wouldn't. So that was evidence all on its own of who had the power here.

The evening was so lovely, the setting sun turning the sky muted orange tinged with blue as darkness consumed what remained of the day.

Had it only been a day? It had been the longest day on record.

"I would like a glass of wine," she said.

"It shall be done."

He lifted a hand, and the server appeared immediately. "Yes, sir?"

"My fiancée will have a glass of whatever you recommend. I will have something red. We will take a sample of the menu."

"Of course, sir."

"A sample?" she asked when the waiter vanished.

"I thought you might like to try everything they have to offer. This is one of the most sought-after reservations in all of Athens."

"And you just managed to get it at the last minute?"

"Yes."

"Did someone else lose their table so that you can have it?"

He lifted a shoulder, so unconcerned. "If so, that was the restaurant's decision, and not mine."

"But you have to realize that someone had to rearrange their entire... The restaurant had to rearrange things for you, or someone had to rearrange their dinner plans for you. You don't shuffle around in empty space, commanding whatever you like without affecting people. Just because you aren't connected to others, doesn't mean you don't impact them."

Okay, she didn't really care so much about the situation with the restaurant. Maybe she was just venting her feelings about being caught up in all of this.

"I'm aware of that. I'm not... I understand how the

world works, Verity, and I understand the way that people's relationships work."

"Do you?"

"I do not owe you this explanation," he said, his voice hard. "But I will give it."

"Gee, thanks, Alex."

"You are marrying me, so perhaps you need to know."

"I'd like to," she said, getting exasperated.

"But it is like... I will use Christmas as an example. It never meant anything to me. And no matter how much someone tells me it's magical, or that it makes them feel a certain feeling, I can never have it. What they are talking about is nostalgia. I will never have nostalgia associated with the holiday. It is nothing but bad memories for me, if anything. Mostly, it didn't signify. You cannot take understanding and turn it into feeling. That is how family is for me. It's how friendship is for me. I can understand the purpose of it, I can understand how it functions, and why other people want it. But I don't."

It made such horrible sense that she almost felt guilty for talking to him the way that she had. For being angry.

Because the deeper she got into this part of him, the more she understood that he had not escaped his upbringing unscathed.

No. He was everything he was because of that upbringing. Successful, yes, but also disconnected.

"Romance is the same," he said. "I understand what

it means to other people. But it will never mean that for me."

"You have no issue with sex," she said, her entire face burning as soon as the words left her mouth.

Right then, the waiter reappeared with their wine and a selection of appetizers. Which looked lovely, but she had just made herself feel slightly ill.

Alex took his wine in hand and leaned back in his chair, regarding her coolly. "To me it is a drive like anything else. I eat and enjoy good food, but I don't long for family dinners. That makes sense?"

Sadly. Very sadly it did.

She was honestly annoyed that he was so good at making this understandable.

"You're angry with me," he said, reaching out and putting a small selection of appetizers onto her plate. "I think you're angry with me because you have an argument."

"This is the problem. You know me. And for me, knowing someone means...feeling something. Whether it's distaste or...friendship. You know me, and you don't feel any of that. You just have the benefit of being able to look inside my head without paying the cost of caring. That doesn't seem fair."

"Consider this," he said, his dark eyes nearly glowing in the faltering light. "I have no choice. There is an entire world within this world that I can see, I can understand, but I cannot enter. All the money in the world won't fix that."

There was no pity in his voice; there was no sadness. It was blunt and matter-of-fact. And she found it desperately sad. Was that just something he had to accept? That circumstances in his childhood had robbed him of something he could never get back?

But then she thought about her own, and the things she had accepted she wouldn't have. That she didn't want a husband and children because being in a family unit had been such a terrible thing for her. She didn't let herself feel wistful about it. Because the institution of family wasn't something that made her feel...warm or happy. Maybe it was the same for him.

Everything was so disconnected from what it was supposed to be, so you couldn't long for it the way that other people did.

She thought about saying that to him, but instead she took a bite of a small cracker in front of her and moaned with delight as the freshness of the fish and radishes on top hit her palate. Maybe it was just better to exist in the moment. Maybe this was the problem. She was so focused on trying to rationalize this moment, fix something, feel better, when maybe she just needed to live in it.

She was hardly being tortured, after all.

She took a sip of her wine, and surrendered. There was no further action to be taken in the conversation unless she was going to start tearing strips of her own skin off and revealing all the issues she had underneath. And that would be silly, because they weren't friends. Because he was her boss. She might as well just stay Verity as he knew her. Because the Verity he knew was always together, always well-adjusted and fine. There had been a little bit less of that over the past week given the whole…everything, but she didn't need to go showing him her soft white underbelly.

"This is beautiful," she said.

He looked at her, his eyes meeting hers, then drifting to her mouth, down to her breasts, which made her nipples go tight, and her stomach feel fluttery. Then back up in her eyes. He was so gorgeous. And dangerous. They had just had a conversation about why he was especially dangerous. He was her boss, he knew her, he didn't feel anything for her.

Unfortunately, her particular brand of trauma hadn't made her disconnect from people. In fact, she wanted connection, just something that looked different from what she'd had growing up. The idea that she could have someone in her life who wanted her around, who appreciated what she did…

She took another long sip of her wine. Oh. Alex was that relationship. He wanted her around, even if it was in a professional capacity. He liked the things that she did, and he was quick to praise her.

It was easy for her to assume that she kept the peace with him, and managed him so well because of her ability to read impending dark moods, and her motivation to avoid them. But it was more than that. It wasn't enough for her to avoid his ire; the past two years she had been existing on his praise.

She had all these thoughts about friendships she might make. About dates she might go on, but she hadn't done that, had she? Because Alex was fulfilling this role in her life that meant so much to her. Because she was actually consumed by her relationship with him.

Thankfully, a lovely course of pasta came out on the heels of that realization, and she was able to take another sip of wine and finish the glass, and chase the thought away.

Music began to play, live guitars, and some of the couples around them got up and started dancing beneath the string lights on the roof.

If she weren't here with a man who had a brick in his chest where his heart should be, it might've been romantic. Of course, it would've been dangerous. Emotionally. They were both the problem.

She could see that very clearly. She had been allowing her boss to fulfill something in her emotionally that a boss shouldn't be fulfilling, and she was now angry at him for not reciprocating.

She was also angry at him for the whole convenient marriage thing, which in fairness to her was absolutely stepping over a line, but still.

"Dance with me," he said, his eyes burning into hers, the statement emphatic, and in no way a request.

Her heart jumped in her chest because it had not gotten the memo that this wasn't romantic.

They were supposed to be performing. She couldn't say no.

So when he extended his hand, she took it. And when he lifted her from her seat and onto her feet she felt like she was flying. He wrapped his arm around her waist and swept her to the dance floor, and any protests or sharp comments she wanted to make were swallowed up by the feeling swelling in her chest. Overwhelming. Brilliant. Beautiful. Horrible.

He pulled her in to his chest, one hand clasping hers, the other wrapped firmly around her waist. She put her hand on his shoulder; she was reasonably sure that was what you were supposed to do when you were dancing. She had never really done it before. If doing it alone in your bedroom didn't count, that was.

He took the lead, strong and steady, and took the guesswork out of everything. His confident steps made her own move easily. Helped her find her rhythm.

The music wrapped itself around them like an intimate veil, and it was as if they were the only two people on the roof. Her heart was pounding, and it wasn't from physical exertion. His body was hot against hers, and she realized she had never been so close to another person before.

It was easier, for some reason, to admit that she had fallen into the trap of getting emotional validation from him, than to admit that she was attracted to him. That she had been attracted to him from the first moment they had met, and that Stavros was a bad decoy for the better, more reasonable aspect of herself that would have screeched an alarm about Alex if she hadn't distracted it.

It had been him. From the beginning. And she was so dedicated to her self protection that she had done her best to hide it from her higher self so that her lower self could have what he wanted.

And now he was holding her. Carrying her across the dance floor like she wasn't a burden. Like he had been born to do it.

If he was so dangerous then why did she fit in his arms like this?

Why did her body feel both relaxed and on edge because of his touch? Why did she feel cherished and safe and electrified all at once?

You don't have a trademark on delusion, Verity. Your feelings aren't facts.

That was true.

But she wasn't like Alex. She had feelings. She just squished them down. Manipulated them. Hid them. Didn't let herself happen. And in effect, it was like she was still letting her parents keep her from having nice things. Or was it protection? It was a question she was having a difficult time answering. Especially while she was in Alex's arms.

There were other people around them, but she didn't have a sense for them. She didn't care about them. This wasn't a performance anymore, not for her. This was her, sorting out her own feelings with fear and trembling. This was her, indulging herself while punishing herself, and examining the punishment.

She sensed something dangerous in Alex, and she had from the beginning. She knew what it was. He would never have feelings for her. It wasn't a great mystery. But she didn't want a forever sort of love anyway, so what did it matter? Except she knew it did, because it hurt her that he didn't consider them friends, so she couldn't even imagine the cost if she were to sleep with him and then...

Her heart started to beat erratically. This was the closest she had come to admitting that she wanted him like that. She looked up at him, her eyes landing first on the sharp cut of his jaw, the curve of his lips, that blade-straight nose. His black lashes, and his dark, fathomless eyes.

She knew why people were afraid of him. Hell, she was afraid of him. For very good reason. She really did need to find a new therapist, because there was something happening here. All this fear, and yet she was drawn to the fearsome thing. Wanted to reach out and touch it, tame it, make it her own.

And she knew she couldn't do that.

He would dominate. He would force submission. Because that was who he was; she wasn't going to be the one...

And anyway, he didn't want her.

She thought of the way that he had looked when she had come out of the dressing room in the pink dress. And then, the way that he had looked at her breasts at the table. Maybe he did. But it was in a base way. It had nothing to do with who she was as a person. It had nothing to do with her.

Do you need it to be?

She didn't know how to answer that question. One

posed by herself, to herself. What kind of sad idiot didn't know herself to this degree?

She knew all her warning signs, all her triggers. But that was different than actually knowing what she wanted and why. It was different than being honest about what she was feeling. She was good at building fences and observing the boundaries. She was not good at reevaluating those boundaries around existing feelings.

She was good at making rules and following them.

Alex had nothing to do with her rules.

He never had. If she had an ounce of real self-preservation inside of her, or even self-awareness, she probably wouldn't have continued working for him, much less said yes to all of this. But right now it felt like a tangle. Wanting to continue to please him and wanting to keep herself safe. But also wanting to continue to be near him.

He moved his hand, and it drifted down her back making her shiver. This was dangerous. So very dangerous.

The worst part was, she was sure she was feeling alone. Just like the sense of friendship, just like—

Her thoughts were interrupted when he swept her around the corner on the dance floor, and backed her up against a vine-covered wall, his dark eyes burning. Her breath caught, her heart slamming hard against her breastbone.

He pressed her hand to the wall, his fingers still laced between hers, and he touched the engagement ring there, a look of something like reverence on his face. She had never seen him look like this before. There was fire in his eyes, something like the expression she had found there when he had seen her in the dress just an hour ago, but also something more.

Something confused, hunted, ravenous.

It mirrored the feelings that were inside of her, finally. Finally it wasn't only her. Who felt like a victim of this thing, who felt like she was at its mercy.

Was he feeling all of this conflicting attraction? This need to embrace it and turn away all at once? This desperate desire to know what it would be like to touch, to taste?

She felt overwhelmed by it, swamped with it, like it might drown her.

He was a man with experience, and she was nothing more than his virgin secretary. That was the tragic fact of it all. She was a stereotype. Ripe for the picking, even. If she tried to explain it to someone, they would scoff. They would say she was being taken advantage of. They would say she was a fool. But they didn't know what it felt like. And they couldn't.

She knew. And judging by the look in his eyes so did he.

They had stopped. The music kept on playing, and people around the corner were probably still dancing, but they had stopped. Almost like they had frozen time itself. There was nothing but this growing, throbbing need between them. It was so real. It was so…all-encompassing. And then, on the breeze, with her breath, it was over. He moved away from her, pulled her from the wall and swept her back to the dance floor, with no explanation, no commentary, nothing.

She took a breath, a gasp, really, and only then did she realize she hadn't been breathing at all.

"Alex..."

"It looks as if the meat course has been served. Would you like another drink?"

He took her hand and led her back to the table, and her head was swimming.

Maybe this was a gift. Maybe it was a reprieve. A chance to make a better choice, instead of giving into... whatever that was. She wanted to say something. She wanted to push.

But something stopped her. Held her back. The same old things.

The fear of what would happen if she pushed at the wrong time.

She was tired of herself. Tired of how much she didn't know. And she was resentful. Of him. For unmasking so much inside of her that was still so broken. It was so easy for her to look at him and have thoughts about his trauma. About his coping mechanisms, and his protections and layers, but looking at her own was just...

She just wanted to be fine.

That was why she had come to Greece. To be fine. To start living.

Maybe when all this was over she finally could.

Maybe it wasn't enough to run away from her family. She needed to run away from Alex too.

And once this was done, she would have the means to do it.

Until then…

She would just plan the wedding. Look at it as another part of the job.

They weren't friends.

And whatever she had seen in his eyes before, she would ignore it.

Because God knew he would.

CHAPTER SEVEN

THE WEDDING CAME upon them quite quickly, and Alex did not think Verity was as appreciative of all he was doing for her as she ought to be. Not only was this a spectacular affair, not only was her name being plastered across the headlines in only glowing terms, but he had done a Herculean job of reining in his attraction to her.

He paused in his room, looking at himself in the mirror, clothed in the tuxedo he would be wearing to the wedding in less than an hour.

Verity was beautiful. He had been conscious of that from the moment he'd hired her. The way he was affected by her beauty had been different. At least initially. There was something young and fresh about her that he had responded to that first day. Something that made him want to protect her. Her beauty—he had told himself—had been something like a lovely figurine he wanted to collect.

Being with her outside of the office—confronting the idea that she might go on a date with someone else—had been taking that figurine and making her flesh and blood. And then it was difficult to avoid the truth that they could only ever see her that way as long as no one else was touching her. As long as he wasn't touching her.

When they had danced at the rooftop bar, he had been so close to taking her in his arms and claiming her. But it wouldn't have stopped at a kiss. He knew that. All too well.

So he had not kissed her. He had turned away from the moment, as he must. All of their outings had since then been confined to holding hands. And she seemed... subdued. Not quite herself.

Almost as if she was angry at him, and yet she never showed such an emotion.

Not his cricket. She seemed as placid and smooth as ever, like the surface of a lake, and the harder he stared, the more he could only see himself looking back. Perversely, it made him more attracted to her. It made him want to create a reaction in her.

He did not.

He was her boss. And while he felt no guilt over using her for this particular endeavor, he was aware of the complexity of it. She had very little choice in the matter. Taking advantage of her physically on top of it would be reprehensible.

He cared about that. He always had. Perhaps because so much of his life had been determined by the whims and failures of other people. He hadn't lied to her when he'd said that he understood the way that human connection worked. He understood all too well. When other people had control over you they could make your life as wonderful or miserable as they wanted to make it. When you had nothing, it gave every meal, every night's rest, every breath a greater weight. And often, you had to observe the rules of a game in order to ensure you would continue to have those things.

It was one reason getting as far away as he could from that state was so important to him. But he would never, ever intentionally put someone else in that position. And in some ways, he had with Verity. He had changed the rules of the job. And the outcome was that he would give her financial freedom, but he had flexed his power over her in a way that he was not proud of.

He wasn't redirecting either.

The wedding was today, and it was going ahead.

The one thing he couldn't do was cross that physical line.

Not and live with himself.

He opted to walk to the ruin where they would be getting married. It was a long walk, but he was in need of some time to clear his head. To gain control over his desires. He was on the cusp of getting what he wanted professionally; why images of Verity should dominate his thoughts was beyond him.

When he arrived at the outskirts of the venue, he looked up and stopped. There she was, sitting in the window on the third floor, her long blond hair blowing in the wind. She was wearing a robe of some kind, and was staring out pensively. She was like a medieval maiden, the sort that knights wrote poetry about. Untouchable and glorious.

His chest felt sore. His heart was beating faster. An old feeling swept through him on the wind. This feeling of wanting without being able to have. It wasn't nostalgia. Not in the way people spoke about it. Not like Christmas as a child. He resented it. Hated it. He was never supposed to want what he couldn't have again. And here he was, standing three floors below his assistant with his heart nearly beating out of his chest.

She wished that when she saw him it didn't make her heart almost explode. But if she could have her way where Alex was concerned, she would be in an entirely different situation right now.

She had opted to have no one help her get ready today. She was putting it off, sitting at the edge of the window and looking down at the glorious view. And that was when he had appeared, like this was some kind of fairy tale and she could let down her hair and he could climb up and... Rescue her? From what? Himself? That was unlikely.

She pretended she didn't see him, or at least she didn't acknowledge his presence before standing up and turning away. She took her robe off and stared at herself in the full-length mirror. The underwear that had been chosen for her to go with the wedding dress was... beautiful and definitely designed for someone to see them. A strapless corset made of white lace and a white lace thong that barely covered anything at all.

Of course, no one would be seeing these.

She told herself that didn't make her ache with regret. She told herself that she could run away if she wanted to. That she didn't have to go through with this. And then she told herself it really wasn't that big of a deal. It was just a ceremony. She wouldn't even know anyone here. It would be media and potential investors, and all of Alex's colleagues. Hers too, of course, but they weren't really hers. In the sense that of course their real loyalty was to the man who wrote their paychecks, and not to her.

But that should make everything easier. This was all part of a life she would leave behind. She had thought things would go differently. She had thought this would be the place where she would settle in, make space for herself. But it wasn't going to be. And that was fine. She didn't care about marriage.

She told herself that repeatedly as she put her dress on. As she scrunched and then fluffed her curls, as she put her minimal makeup on and picked up the glorious bouquet of pale pink roses that were sitting there waiting for her.

She didn't have any bridesmaids. Just as Alex didn't have any groomsmen. Did anything speak more profoundly about the two of them than that? She took a breath, and looked at her reflection one last time before she turned away and began to walk for the door. The place they were getting married at was glorious. And if she was ever going to plan a wedding, it probably would have looked like this.

She giggled. To no one, and really nothing, but it was silly to think she would have ever been able to have a wedding like this without Alex.

Was she already getting used to the things that came with being attached to a billionaire?

Financially, her family had always been comfortable enough. Not wealthy, but they'd had stability externally. A nice enough house on a nice enough street. It was only inside that things had been rotten. Still, a fabulous wedding at a glorious Grecian ruin would have been beyond them.

But if it was just a fantasy, and she could have whatever she could dream of, she would have dreamed of this. The facility she'd gotten ready in was essentially a castle, the winding staircase leading down to a courtyard that had once been a library. Now it was half-crumbled walls and pillars, which had been decked in roses and lights, a grand arbor standing between two of the most intact pillars.

And she could see as she peered through the windows on her way down the spiraling staircase, that that courtyard was now filled with guests sitting in the golden chairs that had been set out in the vast space. She was making false vows in front of strangers. And maybe the Greek gods. But they would enjoy the farce, honestly. So she didn't need to worry about that either. Surely Zeus could appreciate marital shenanigans.

She swallowed hard. This was the best decision. It was.

When she arrived down at the base of the staircase

the doors parted for her, and the sun shone upon her. Like a sign from above. So she pressed forward, out into the gloriously beautiful day, and toward her husband.

Music played by a string quartet filtered around her, the same song they had danced to at the rooftop bar, but surely that was a coincidence. Her heart began to beat faster. She could see him now, standing there at the head of the altar looking resplendent in that black tuxedo. Her glimpse of him out the window from that distance hadn't given her the full story of all that glory.

She was drawn to him, and this no longer felt fake.

A smile spread across her face, and she wished that she could stop it. She couldn't. And then, just as she got to the end of the aisle, she turned, and saw her mother.

Next to her was Verity's father. Her brother was next to him, and right beside her brother was her sister.

And suddenly everything stopped. Her heart, the world, that strange sensation of joy that had made her feel like everything was going to be okay. And suddenly, it felt like there were eggshells beneath her feet, like every step risked breaking something essential.

She didn't want to look at them. She kept on looking at Alex. She knew that she looked affected. There was nothing she could do about it. She couldn't speak. And when they joined hands at the altar, his were like fire.

Or perhaps her own had turned to ice.

CHAPTER EIGHT

HE COULD SEE the exact moment when her entire countenance changed. She had seen her family sitting in the front row of the wedding, and it was like all the life had been drained from her.

He had thought it would be a given that her family would come to the wedding. When he had turned over the task of who to invite to one of the administrators in the office, he had told her to include people who might be connected to Verity. She had been like a robot throughout the entire ceremony, and then had gone into hiding for about fifteen minutes before finally appearing at the reception.

She had a sparkling smile on her face, but there was something odd about it. Something frozen and stuck, not her usual applied neutrality, but a sort of manic false joy that made him feel ill at ease.

The guests, however, did not seem aware of the situation.

When she joined him at their banquet table, he leaned in toward her. "Is something wrong?"

"Of course not," she said. "Nothing is wrong."

He could see that half her focus was devoted to watching her family. They didn't approach the table, nor did they socialize with other guests. But he supposed they were very much out of place at the event. Nearly everyone was a business contact of his, and the primary language being spoken around the room was Greek so it was not entirely strange that her family might be keeping to themselves.

"You're welcome to mingle," he said.

She laughed. "Am I? Well, that's fantastic. I wasn't certain what the rules were."

"Rules?"

"Yes. Rules. Of course there are rules." She lowered her voice. "This is your game, not mine, and I'm not a real bride."

"Be careful," he said, warning her because it was very important they didn't disrupt the facade, but part of him found that wasn't even his primary concern. She was acting strangely, but he couldn't pinpoint why, and he found that disconcerting.

"Yes. Of course. I don't think you have any idea how careful I'll be for the whole rest of the evening."

Dinner was served, and she spent the entire meal eating while staring blandly ahead with the same sort of serene smile on her face. As soon as she was finished, she stood up and made her way over to her family's table. Her posture was straight, her smile only growing brighter. She laughed too loudly at everything her brother said, and every time her father asked for something she moved quickly to see it done.

He had a steady stream of well-wishers moving to speak to him, but he finally excused himself and made his way over to Verity's family. "Pleased to meet you," he said. "I'm Alex."

"It's very nice to meet you," said Verity's mother. "I'm Dorothy. It's shocking, really, that Verity has found herself in such a grand position."

"Is it?" he asked.

"Well, she was such a terribly average child. When she took off to Greece it was a surprise."

The smile on Verity's face looked like it might shatter. "It surprised me too. But opportunity was calling. And apparently Alex. Everything worked out exactly like it was supposed to. Amazing."

"You could always thank your old man for paying for your college," her dad said. It was not spoken with familial warmth, and Alex didn't need to be an expert on family to recognize that.

"Of course I'm grateful," Verity said. "I am exceedingly thankful for everything you've done for me. All of you. Without you I wouldn't be here. Of course. Marrying Alex. Which is my dream come true."

The doors opened, and revealed a cake on a rolling cart being brought over to the banquet table.

"Excuse us," Verity said. "It's time to cut the cake."

She cut the cake with the same sort of manic energy she was doing everything else. After that it was time for them to dance, and where there had been an erotic edge to their touching the last time he'd held her in his arms, it didn't exist now. She was practically vibrating with unrest. After the dance, she went back to her family, where she spent the rest of the evening. It was like watching a vaudevillian show. She was performing with so much effort that he could feel the force of it from across the room.

He knew that anyone else would just think she was smiling, happy even. But this wasn't Verity. He knew her. He could feel her.

And he also knew enough to know this wasn't a terribly normal family dynamic, but he couldn't read exactly what it was either. It took him an hour to realize she was counting the amount of drinks her mother and father were having, and attempting to slow the amount of alcohol being served to them.

He wondered if the issue was she was afraid they would recognize that this wasn't a real relationship. That they weren't a real couple. Nobody knew Alex, but of course her family knew her.

Nothing happened. Not a single outburst or moment of unpleasantness. And soon, the wedding was over, and it was time for the two of them to go up to the honeymoon suite. It was a room large enough for him to take his space and her to have hers. As soon as they walked out of the ballroom, cheers echoing behind them, and entered the foyer of the castle, at the foot of the stairs, she pulled away from him.

"What is it?"

"How dare you?" She spoke in a voice that wasn't familiar to him. It was vibrating with rage, low and trembling.

"How dare I what?"

"You invited my family to the wedding, and you didn't ask me. You didn't tell me. I wasn't prepared."

"I'm sorry. If you are afraid that they might identify that this wasn't—"

"You think I'm worried about the fake wedding?" She laughed. "I'm not worried about that. And believe me, they would never be able to identify whether this was real or not. They would have to have the slightest bit of insight into me, and I guarantee you they don't."

They reached the top of the stairs, and she stormed ahead, pushing open the door to the bridal suite, and slamming the door in his face. He caught it with his hand and pushed it open. "Tell me what the problem is."

"The problem is that you don't know me. At all. And not only that, you haven't even taken the slightest bit of effort to get to know me. If you had, then you would know that my mother, father, brother and sister being here is quite literally my worst nightmare." She shook her head. "It doesn't matter how much I try, does it? I was so afraid to be angry at you. I'm so afraid to be angry at anyone. I spent the entire night performing to try and make them happy. I left this behind, I wasn't supposed to have to do it again. I wasn't ready to. There were digs every few minutes. About how this is above me, and now I'm above them, about what I owed them. And I just have to take it on the chin. I have to pretend that I don't hear it." She took a deep breath, and tried to steady herself.

Then she continued. "You don't have a family, so you don't understand what a nightmare they can be."

"You didn't tell me you had an issue with your family," he said, surprised that her mention of his lack sparked his temper the way that it did. "It seemed like an entirely reasonable thing to make sure they were invited."

"If they're around then I can guarantee I will spend the entire time trying to keep my feelings from getting hurt, while I try to keep them from making a scene. If my parents end up drinking, then they will end up screaming at each other. Or a waiter. Or someone who happens to look at them wrong. Though, usually it's me. Because my brother and sister learned how to fight back, and I spent all of my time trying to fix everything. That makes me the referee. It makes me everything that I don't want to be. And this is why I have to live in a different country. This is why I…"

She stood there, breathing hard, her breasts rising and falling with the motion. And suddenly, she threw her head back and let out a feral scream. "This is why I'm scared to have any feeling that isn't…conciliatory." She shook her head. "This is why I didn't have your head for getting me involved in this…this farce. I can't believe you did this. I can't believe you railroaded me into it. You used the promise of financial freedom to lure me here. And for what? So you can have more. More and more. I don't matter to you at all. You could've asked any random woman who passed you on the street to pretend to be your wife and it would've worked just as well."

"That isn't true," he said. "Everyone loves you."

He knew immediately that was the wrong thing to say. Even if he didn't know why. Because her face turned red.

"Yes. Everyone loves me. Because I have a lifetime of practice at making everyone else happy. I have a lifetime of managing all that. And I turned around and I did it with you. I do it with everyone at the company. I do it all the time. And I can't... I don't even know who I am. I'm afraid of the stupidest things. Scared to make a mistake. Scared to make people angry. I'm always walking on my tiptoes. I'm tired of it. I can't do this anymore."

Her breathing got faster and faster. "I can't... I can't breathe." She reached around behind herself and she unzipped the wedding dress, tearing at it, shoving it down to the floor, leaving her standing there in nothing but white lace undergarments that left little to the imagination.

It was a rare thing for Alex to be surprised. But this had caught him entirely off guard, and he had no idea what he was supposed to do now. Another rarity.

"What has it gotten me?" she asked, standing there in half-naked fury, her blond hair a wild ride around her shoulders, her breasts rising and falling with each outraged breath. "Absolutely nothing. Saddled with this ridiculous situation, and I don't matter. Not to anyone. My parents came to seek spectacle, undoubtedly they came to see if they could get any money from you. Or maybe they just wanted to make this difficult for me. Maybe they don't even know that they make things difficult for me. Maybe they've never thought about my perspective even one time." She laughed. "I think that's it. I think they never thought even one time about how they made me feel. Exactly like you."

She shook her head. "You never think about how I feel."

Anger galvanized him now. He growled, and moved toward her. "That's not true. I didn't coerce you into this. You agreed."

"You released a statement before you ever spoke to me."

"What have I asked of you?"

"You asked me to marry you. You forced me to."

"I offered you good money to marry me, and if you didn't want the money, you could've said no."

"Everyone wants the money. And now you see why I wanted it. It's to never have to go back to that. Ever."

"There's a lot of space between that and the sort of riches that I've given you. Don't turn me into the enemy because you're angry at your father."

"Oh I'm plenty angry at him, and I know well that I am. But I'm angry at you too."

"You have given me no credit for all that I've done for you. For the way that I protected you."

"Protected me? Protecting me would have been to ask the basic question of whether or not I had moved halfway across the world to get away from my parents, rather than just making assumptions."

"Yes, I have protected you."

"How?" She took a step toward him, all fire and

glory. "By bringing my worst nightmare to me on my fake wedding day?"

It was his turn to move toward her, and he had been paying attention to where they were in the room, but it brought her back up against one of the ornately carved wooden posts on the stately canopy bed at the center of the room.

"Yes," he ground out. "I have protected you. I did my level best to keep this as professional as possible."

"You married me."

"You know what I mean," he said, all restraint flooding out of him. She had no idea. He was not the sort of man who wanted something and didn't get it. No. That had been his entire childhood, and as an adult he didn't do that. With her, he had made an exception. With her, he had observed best practices. He had been a good man where she had been concerned, and she was acting like he was the very monster from the Black Lagoon for bringing her parents to see her.

"No. I don't."

He lifted his hand, and reached out and touched her face. Dragging his finger slowly along her cheekbone, down to her jaw. That silenced her. She drew a sharp breath, her eyes going glossy. "You don't know?"

"No," she whispered.

"Then I will have to show you."

And then he lowered his head and claimed her mouth with his own.

CHAPTER NINE

HER THOUGHTS WERE a whirlwind wrapped in a sensual haze. She couldn't make sense of anything. A moment ago she had been yelling at Alex, and now he was kissing her.

Even more confusing, a moment ago she had stripped her dress off with him in the room.

Like she hadn't thought this would be the end result.

Well, she hadn't been thinking at all. She'd been feeling. She had been ready to come out of her skin, and was tired, so desperately tired of having to make everything palatable. Having to make herself palatable. Her feelings were confused and sharp and she wanted him to feel them. She didn't want to hide them.

So she kissed him back. Deep and long, pouring every ounce of her anger, of her hurt, of the impossible to define, spiky feelings that she couldn't even put names to, that attached themselves to her heart like barbs, hellish and painful, and impossible to dig out.

Kissing him seemed to make her feel better. Or if not better, seemed to make her feel something else. Something more. Something good mixed in with all of the bad. It was intense; she hadn't been wrong. She had known that this was the sort of connection that could consume her. The sort of attraction that could crash over her like a tsunami and claim her. She was jumping into it now. Without thought, without reserve.

He thought he had been protecting her by not kissing her? It was probably the best thing he had done in the last month. She would tell him that, when she decided to come up for air. But for now, she was reveling in this.

The heat of his mouth, the expert slide of his tongue against hers, the way that his large hands moved over her body, the way that he gripped her hips, and pulled her toward him so that she could feel the burgeoning length of his arousal. She might be a virgin, but she knew how it all worked. She wasn't afraid.

Because she had to face down her biggest fear. She hadn't even realized that this specific thing was her biggest fear, but if she had really sat down and thought about it she would have said that having her family at her actual wedding would have been her worst nightmare. And she would've also said that it would only happen in her nightmares, because there was no way she would ever get married, and no way she would invite her family if she did.

But here she was, married to this man. And her family had been there.

She hadn't died, but she had felt damn near close to it.

What could scare her after this?

Certainly not his kiss, which was expert and drugging. Glorious and all-consuming. Certainly not his kiss, her first, the greatest. She was so glad she had gone on a date with Stavros, because would she have given him this? Would she have surrendered her lips to him, her body, when it was so clear that this belonged to Alex?

That it had from the moment she had first met him.

What Verity was good at, very good at, was not just smoothing things over for everyone else, but for herself. She was so good at avoiding difficult feelings, and the truth about herself. But not now.

She was just admitting it, even if it was internal.

She wanted Alex.

She had from the very first moment she had laid eyes on him. She had wanted to be near him. Every moment that she could be. She had wanted him like this. Even if she couldn't allow herself to so much as fantasize about it in the dead of night. But it was so easy now. It felt so right now. Because on some level she had always known.

He pulled away from her, and she leaned back against the bedpost, breathing hard. Her lips felt hot and swollen; her breasts felt heavy. That place between her legs was wet and throbbing, and needy. She wanted him to touch her. When she had thought about her first time, she had imagined that it would be awkward. That she wouldn't know what she wanted, that she would feel hesitant. That wasn't true. Not at all. She knew exactly what she wanted. And she wasn't ashamed.

"Take your clothes off," she said, clutching the post for emotional and physical support as she watched him.

"Will that satisfy your anger?"

"It depends on how much I like what I see."

"I'm not concerned," he said, reaching for the knot on his tie.

Just then she felt like she was existing in two different spaces and times. Like she was watching him in his position at his desk, eating his usual lunch, then angrily eating a salad, and then she was back here. Watching him loosen the knot on his tie, watching him deftly unbutton his shirt. Same man. It was a very difficult process.

It was getting harder and harder to breathe. Especially as he revealed more and more of his toned, glorious chest. Covered in dark hair, and sculpted like a work of classical art. Oh goodness. He was getting naked.

She had asked him to.

No, she had demanded it.

She wasn't afraid. She was just a little bit in awe that it was happening. But that wasn't the same as being afraid.

He stripped off his shirt, his jacket, let it all fall to the floor. She was speechless, her mouth dry. He had muscles in places she didn't even know men had muscles. Definition all down that ridged abdomen, and glorious cuts that created an arrow leading her eye down to the waistband of his pants. His hands went to the buckle of his belt, and he began to undo it slowly, his methodical movements maddening.

She had a feeling he knew it. She kept holding onto the bed.

Because if she didn't she might fall to pieces. Because if she didn't she might melt into a puddle. Because if she didn't, maybe she would just fall over, like an imbalanced quail that couldn't stand on its own two feet.

She refused to be a tilting bird. She would not tip over. She didn't trust herself, though, so she gripped even more tightly to the carved wood, her nails scraping against the surface.

She watched with rapt attention as he removed the rest of his clothes, and she did feel lightheaded at the first glimpse she got of a fully naked man in the flesh.

And what a naked man he was.

She had seen quite a lot of naked male statues about Greece in the last few years, and as their masculinity could be easily hidden by fig leaves, it had never seemed like much to write home about, if Verity would write home about anything. Alex would not be able to be concealed by a single fig leaf. Not even close.

And there were the virginal nerves. The ones that she had thought she had perhaps dodged. Right on time. But thankfully, the bedpost held her upright, and so she didn't falter or collapse.

"I have done as you commanded, Cricket. Is there a reward for me?"

"I...am thinking about it."

She was racking her brain trying to come up with what might be an equivalent reward.

"I think perhaps it is your turn to remove your clothing."

She blinked. "That isn't an equivalent trade."

"Why?"

"Because you are... You look like that."

"I can practically see all there is to see of you now, Cricket. I'm confident that what you have to reveal is better."

This was even better than getting a compliment at work. She was tempted to try and get more. Oh, she was so very tempted. With shaking knees, she released her hold on the bedpost, reached behind her back and began to undo the clips on the corset. Then, on a swift and drawn breath she let it drop to the ground, revealing the upper half of her body.

He made a short, masculine sound of approval in the back of his throat that sent her heartbeat into overdrive. And it was the approval she needed to take the rest of her clothing off.

"Yes," he said. "That's right. You're a beautiful girl. Do you know how beautiful you are? I have never seen such glory."

This time, when her knees went weak it was with pleasure. She could see that he was telling the truth. The way that he was looking at her didn't lie. He was aroused, yes, but it was more than that. He approved of her. He was looking at her and finding her to be enough. To be perfect.

She would give him anything he wanted. Right then, she really thought she would.

She would live under his desk in his office, rest her head on his thigh while he worked, be on hand to fetch things for him, whatever, as long as he would look at her like that.

"Such a good girl," he said, those words the final arrow in any resistance that might have remained.

She was his. He had seen into her, and she had been afraid of that. The way that he knew her, the way that he understood her, almost better than she understood herself, without giving any of himself. But right now it didn't matter.

Couldn't this just be about her? Her getting everything she wanted? Her having her every fantasy realized?

He thought she was beautiful.

And after today, after having to manage her family like that, didn't she deserve something nice?

He might have delivered her worst nightmare to her doorstep, but now he was giving her the deepest, dearest fantasy she'd never quite known she had. It was terrifying. It made her quake inside and out.

Would she have slept with someone a lot earlier if she had realized? If she had realized what it would make her feel for a man to praise her like this?

No. The answer echoed inside of her, whispered through her with total certainty. Because just anyone's praise wouldn't mean anything. It had to be Alex. Because he was so exacting, so difficult.

She wanted to please him. She wanted to please him because doing so meant something. Healed something inside of her. So she would let herself have it.

Tonight, she would let herself have it, and damn the consequences.

"Sit on the bed," he commanded. And she wanted to do what she was told. She didn't feel like he was taking something from her by taking command. She felt like he was giving her the opportunity to give him everything he wanted, to let her please him, and she wanted that more than anything. That was pleasing herself, and maybe she would never be able to untangle that and make it make sense to somebody else, but she didn't need it to.

It made sense to her.

Or maybe it didn't. Maybe it just felt good. That was enough. For now, that was enough.

"Lay down, and spread your legs, let me get a good look at you."

Her exacting boss was exactly like she should have imagined he would be in bed. She hadn't let herself, because she had been too afraid, because she had been too deep in denial, but of course this was how he was.

He was a man who knew exactly what he wanted, and gave explicit instruction on how he might get it.

And she was the woman who did his bidding. So she did now.

She parted her thighs, and ignored a rush of heat that flooded her cheeks.

"I never thought that I would get married, much less have a wedding night. But you are certainly making a case for why I was foolish in neglecting such a pleasure. Of course, no other woman would do, not like this."

Her thighs began to tremble. His words were amping up her pleasure in a way she had never imagined possible. When he touched her, all was lost. She would be lost. She wasn't afraid of it; she was anticipating it. She needed it.

"Touch yourself," he said. "Show me what you like."

She sucked in a sharp breath, nerves overtaking her now. She wanted to do it right. She wanted to arouse him. She wanted—

"You cannot do it wrong," he said. "Nothing that you do could ever be wrong. Not here."

She bit her lip and nodded slowly, brought one hand up to cup her breast, moved her own thumb over her tightened nipple, her hips arching up off the bed as pleasure arrowed through her. He was watching her with rapt attention, and she kept her eyes on his as she moved her other hand down between her legs and pushed her fingers through her slick folds. White-hot pleasure lanced through her as she stroked herself beneath his intent gaze.

Her hips canted up off the bed in time with her movements, her breathing shortening, coming faster, harder.

"Stop," he said.

She froze.

"You're not allowed to make yourself come. Only I get to do that. And now I have seen just how. You are beautiful when you pleasure yourself. Now let's see how beautiful you are when I pleasure you."

He moved to the bed, his wide shoulders between her thighs as he forced them farther apart, gazing intently at that most intimate part of her. Then he lowered his head and licked her, long and slow.

She gasped, desire nearly pulling her apart. He moved his thumb to where his lips had just been, and stroked her where she was most sensitive, rolling pleasure moving through her like a wave. And then his mouth was on her again as he pushed a finger inside of her making her entirely incoherent.

He pleasured her like that until she was begging. Until she had no more control over herself.

He moved up her body, pressing his forehead to hers, his mouth just a whisper away. She could smell her own arousal on his lips, the realization making her shiver. "Beautiful," he whispered. "Perfection."

"I take the pill," she said. She was on it for her cycle, but she figured she might as well use it for its intended purpose.

She trusted him. She knew him well enough to know that he was fastidious in all things, and that if there was any doubt they couldn't do this safely, he wouldn't.

But he took her words as she meant them, pressing himself inside of her on one smooth thrust. She cried out, the shock at the invasion almost making her fly off the mattress.

"Cricket?" he asked, his voice rough.

"I'm okay," she said. "It just surprised me. Please. I... I wanted to be good for you. I want you to like it. I need you to—"

He silenced her with a kiss, deep and long. Then he smoothed her hair out of her face. "You are perfect. Of course I like this. You fit me perfectly. I only wish I had known so that I hadn't hurt you."

But the pain didn't matter. She had pleased him. That made it all fade away. Made the pleasure rise up inside of her. Made everything turn to glittering gold and glory.

"I'm just fine."

She kissed him, softly, and then he growled and began to move within her, building the pleasure back up inside of her with each decisive stroke.

She clung to him, arching her hips in time with the movement.

This was terrifying. She'd had every good reason to be afraid of this. Because it was intense. Because it was all-consuming. But right now, it was hers. And nothing could take this moment from her. He whispered words of affirmation in her ear, the kind that could never be repeated in polite company, her pleasure building inside of her like a tide, and when it finally flooded through her, she dug her fingernails into his shoulders and called out his name.

"Alex," she whimpered.

All the years, all the lunches, all their time flashed back through her eyes until she came back to this moment. In bed with him, her husband.

He had given her this most beautiful night. This most brilliant gift.

And she realized, with a crushing weight, that while this had changed so much for her, it would have changed absolutely nothing for him.

CHAPTER TEN

Alex didn't sleep. He sat beside the bed, wearing only his tuxedo pants, watching Verity sleep fitfully.

When she shifted and the covers lowered, exposing her breasts, he covered her back up, and when the sun rose he called downstairs to have breakfast brought to them.

He opened up the curtains, and allowed a shaft of light to bathe Verity where she still slept. It had the desired effect. She began to stir, then sat up, rubbing at the sleep in her eyes.

"Breakfast," he said.

He set the tray on the foot of the bed, and she pulled the blankets up to her chin, snuggling deeper into the mattress and closing her eyes purposefully.

"You should eat," he said. "And have coffee."

She opened her eyes and fixed him with the same sort of grumpy look she had given him the day she'd fed him salad. Except this one felt a lot more genuinely outraged.

"I don't need you to tell me what to do," she said.

"Is this how you're going to play this?"

"I'm not playing anything," she said, rolling onto her back and flinging her arm over her eyes. "I don't feel well."

"Are you ill, or are you upset?"

"Does it matter?"

"Yes, it does matter. Because if you feel ill I will have someone fetch you medicine. If you're upset, then I fear you're stuck with me and I'm not well versed in how to handle emotions."

"I thought you understood the workings of humanity and human relationships, you're just above them."

"I'm not above them. I'm outside them. Two different things. I owe you an apology, Verity."

She looked at him then. "For what?"

"That's not..."

"I need to know what you're actually sorry for. I need to know if you have any actual idea what you did. I don't want you to apologize just because you think it's going to make me more...pliant."

"No. That's not why I'm apologizing. I used you badly. I didn't realize how badly until... I didn't know you were a virgin."

"Oh my God," Verity said, sitting up and letting her blankets fall down around her waist. "That's what you're apologizing for? Because you've attached some kind of meaning to...to that? That is the most basic, asinine, male thing you have ever done."

"No," he said, realizing that he was messing this up, and realizing he cared, which was honestly the extraordinary part. He often made people angry, uncomfortable and annoyed. He did not often feel so desperate to fix it. "It's only that it speaks to... I don't know you. Obviously. I spent two years having lunch with you, and I don't know you, and that is a flaw in my system, but you didn't ask to be a victim of that. All of the things you said to me last night are true. I manipulated you into this. I didn't even realize that I did."

"Great. A marriage license and one virginity later and now you have regrets."

"I want to fix this."

"I don't think Scotch tape works on hymens."

"What happened to my biddable assistant?"

"She is now your tired wife who expended all her appeasement energy yesterday on her parents."

"Are you going to be difficult or are you going to have a conversation with me?"

"I've already had the conversation. I was desperately vulnerable and honest with you last night. And you think that you can...express a moment of regret and offer me—well, you really can offer me coffee—and that will make it go away?"

"No. I don't know. I don't know what I can do to fix this. I don't know what I can do..."

"Give me some coffee," she said.

"Okay," he said, reaching for the carafe and pouring a generous mug of hot liquid, handing it to her.

She snatched it away and hoarded it against her chest like a small dragon keeping watch on a precious jewel.

She had told him about herself last night, as she had yelled at him. It was up to him to do more with that, not to ask her to give more, he supposed. Or maybe it was up to him to give something.

"I was five years old when I realized my life wasn't normal." He looked at his hands, then out the window. "When I realized that most children lived in one house, with the same caregivers. Even if it was a grandmother, a single mom, they had stability. Someone who loved them. That kids who were passed around like objects were the strange ones." He felt something catching his chest. "I know many kids in my position spend a lot of time asking themselves why their parents didn't want them. I know little enough about my parents that I'm not sure if they wanted me or not. They could've lost custody because of addiction. Perhaps they did want me. They are a void in my mind. There's nothing there, not enough to grasp onto. Not enough to question. Mainly, I wonder why no one else wanted me. I went into the system when I was an infant. I had the highest chances of being adopted because of that. So many children are taken away from their parents when they're older. People don't want older children. They don't want the trauma that comes with them. They want babies. But nobody wanted me."

He felt very much like he had taken a knife and peeled a layer off of his skin. Exposed something, not just to her, but to himself. "Part of what I did with your parents came from a place of arrogance, I admit. But when you told me that you had lived in one house your entire life, one house growing up, I also admit that I imagined it must've been happy. You are soft, and it seems as if connecting with people is easy for you. I never asked you about your experiences growing up, because I thought that I knew. I thought someone like you must have a good family."

He looked back at her then, and saw that his words had done something to soften her.

"I never thought of that. How...normal it must've seemed to you to move from one place to the next. And what that must've felt like when you realized it wasn't. It must've been confusing."

He nodded. "Yes."

"I can also understand that for you it must feel...ungrateful. Ungrateful of me to have a family, to have a house like that and to have a complicated relationship with those things."

"No," he said. "You forget I lived with a lot of families. Even though they weren't mine, even though I wasn't really a part of them, I have a very clear sense for how every family is different. Some of those families I stayed with were warm and wonderful, and leaving them hurt. Some of them had beautiful dinners every night, and they sat and spoke to each other about their days, and even asked me about mine. Some families are all silent resentment, or everyone in the house bending over backward to placate the member of the family who has a temper. It sounds as if you lived in a house where you were the one who contorted yourself around everyone else."

She sighed. "Yes. I didn't realize how much I did it until I was thirteen. I had a friend over and she said that I acted so different around my family. Strange. Like a robot. She's not wrong. In order to deal with them I learned to sand all the difficult edges off my own feelings and make everything about theirs."

"Were your parents violent with you?"

"No. It's all shouting or… You heard what my mom said. About me being average. That's just normal conversation for her. But if you get her angry…every poisonous thought she's ever had about you will come out of her mouth. And as much as I try to tell myself that it's just her, that it has nothing to do with me, it stings. She's a bitter, unhappy woman. My father is a small, angry man who constantly needs everyone to tell him how important he is. My siblings learned how to trade on that economy. And I just wanted nothing to do with it. I just wanted everything to be as smooth as possible. I just wanted to get through my childhood, and get out on my own."

"You did."

"I did. I went to college, I went to Greece."

"You went to college, but you never dated anyone."

She shook her head. "No. I am nothing if not very protective of myself. That's why I got so angry with you last night. I ran away from this. From all of these hard feelings."

"I didn't know."

"I know. Because I'm protective of myself." She laughed. "Somehow, I protected myself right into this situation." She took a deep breath. "But I did get angry at you. I can't decide if I'm proud of myself for that or not. I can't decide if that makes me like my parents, or if... I finally let myself have all the anger that I wasn't allowed to have in that house full of people who made everything about them."

"There's nothing wrong with being angry," he said.

"If there is then my entire life is a problem." He laughed. "Maybe it is. But I would think that as long as you don't use your anger to hurt other people there's nothing inherently wrong with it. Anyway, I deserve it."

"I can't argue with that."

Silence lapsed between them.

She reached over and picked up a croissant from the tray, and he felt that was a victory of a kind.

"Are you entirely angry with me?"

She wrinkled her nose. "What do you mean by that?"

"I mean, you woke up extremely angry. Is that the only...?" Their eyes caught and held, and he felt desire tightening in his gut. This was such a novel experience, to have slept with a woman he knew so well.

She might argue that he didn't know her, or hadn't before last night, but in the context of his life, he knew her better than he knew most anyone.

So there wasn't just desire, but a strange, fierce feeling of tenderness which was entirely foreign to him.

"Are you wanting to know if I enjoyed what we did last night?"

"I need to know."

"You couldn't tell?"

"Physically, I can tell that you did, but this morning you're upset. I want to know if you regret it."

She looked down. "No. It was a gift to myself. Because I wanted you. Because I have wanted you."

Satisfaction gripped him low and hard.

She narrowed her eyes. "Don't look so pleased with yourself."

"Do I look pleased with myself?"

"You do. I'm still kind of mad at you."

"But you wanted me."

She looked away. And he wanted…he wanted something he didn't have a name for. He wanted to feel connected to her again. As he had last night. When they had made love.

He moved to the edge of the bed, and pressed his knee down on the mattress, then he leaned in and cupped her cheek with his hand. She didn't move away from him. So he leaned in and kissed her softly on the lips.

She whimpered, and went pliant against him. "Alex," she breathed.

"Very good," he whispered. And then she arched against him.

He knew that she liked this. That she craved his praise, but the truth was, he wanted to give it to her. Nothing and no one had ever been his. And she could be. His perfect, beautiful wife. She could belong to him.

The idea of that was intoxicating. She could be his perfect one, adored and kept safe by him. He wanted to give her everything she wanted, to lavish her with jewels and designer dresses, to give her food and beautiful shelter and trips to anywhere in the world she wanted to go.

He had never had anyone to take care of him; it was true. But he had also never had anyone to take care of, and the idea of Verity being his in this way was...

Now that he had taken hold of the idea he couldn't let it go.

He wanted her. Needed her. Craved her like a drug in his system.

He had never wanted another person like this. Sex for him had always been a practicality, as he had said to Verity. Something like being hungry and making sure that he could be satiated.

But there had never been an emotional component, and now there was this, and he was drowning in it. The depth of it. The possibility of it.

He stripped the blankets away from her, took her coffee out of her hand and set the cup on the nightstand.

Then he stripped himself naked and kissed her lips, her neck, down the gorgeous swell of her breasts, down her stomach, to the curls between her legs.

She was addicting. Incredible. He could never get enough of this; he was certain of it. It had altered him fundamentally on some level inside of him he hadn't known existed. And he wanted more. He craved more.

He licked her until she was screaming, until she cried out his name. Then he kissed her inner thigh, pulled away from her and grabbed her chin, tilting her face up toward him. "I want you to do the same for me."

She lowered her eyes, her lashes fanning out over her cheeks. Demure, beautiful. "I don't know how."

"I don't need you to have skill. I simply need you to

be who you are. I want you, I don't want generic pleasure. You, your mouth, your body, that's what I want. You will be perfect, because you are perfect for me."

He watched as color suffused her cheeks, as pleasure overtook her. She loved when he praised her, emotionally, but also he could see that it aroused her. That it satisfied her on so many essential planes. It made him want to give her more. Always.

He stroked her cheek, then released his hold on her. She adjusted their positions so that she was hovering over him, her lips pressed against his shaft.

He groaned, letting his head fall back as she swallowed him down, as she began to pleasure him with all her inexpert ministrations. He loved it. Loved that he could feel that she was learning on him, that she was finding her way with him. She was his.

He hadn't known that connection could make sex better. That this deep yearning need to hang onto a partner and care for her in every way, pleasure her, wrap her in blankets, give her good food, would be the ultimate in satisfaction. But it was.

His Verity. His Cricket.

His.

She pleasured him until he reached the summit, and he pulled her away from him, because he couldn't let it end like this.

"Did I not please you?"

"Yes," he said, pressing his thumb to her lips. "You did. You were perfect. But too good. I don't want to finish like that. Someday I will. And you will swallow all of me, won't you?"

Her cheeks went bright red. "Of course I will."

"Yes. I know you will, because you're so good for me. But now, I need to be inside of you. I need you all around me. Do you understand?"

She nodded, lying back on the bed and arching upward, an invitation that he wasn't going to refuse. "You're so tight and wet," he growled, moving into position. "So perfect for me. And only mine. Do know how much that pleases me?"

She nodded. "Yes. I think I waited for you."

As soon as those words left her mouth, he lost all of his control. He thrust inside of her, the warm welcome of her body pushing him to the edge. His teeth were gritted together, and he fought for any control he might find.

In the end, he could find none, so he surrendered. To her, to this. To the inevitability of it.

He was never going to let her go.

Never.

She was his. His.

His good girl. His wife. His everything.

There was no one else. There was nothing else.

He had found a link, he had found a connection; in this, in this moment, in this feeling, he knew what it was to be joined to another person. To truly have another person he couldn't imagine living without, breathing without.

Too soon, his pleasure overtook him. Too soon, he lost control. "Come for me, beautiful girl," he said.

He was desperate for her to return pleasure, and she did, arching against him and riding out her release, pushing him toward his own.

He clung to the feeling. To the certainty. But it rolled away along with his pleasure, and when it was over, he was just Alex again. And she was Verity. He had lost the connection.

The feeling that had overtaken him.

He sat up, breathing hard, his skin slicked and sweat. He felt like he was coming down from a high, and it was brutal.

He was still trying to find his breath when the words tumbled from his mouth. "It will be impossible to resist you."

"You sound angry about that," she said, shrinking away from him.

He regretted the way he'd spoken but he was still reeling, still dizzy. Still grappling with the way things had changed.

"What will become of us over the next six months?"

Her face went stony. "Right. Because it's still…it's still all about that, isn't it? Your business."

"My goal hasn't changed," he said.

And yet he knew it wasn't that simple.

His goal hadn't changed, but he had. What he wanted, the way he saw the future. He had felt something he hadn't known was possible when he was with her and he didn't want to give it up. Not ever.

"No, of course it hasn't," she said.

"My goal hasn't changed, but my vision of this marriage has. You didn't want to get married, I understand that. But you can be angry with me, you discovered that last night. I won't force you to change the shape of yourself to keep peace. And I... Verity, what if you and I could have a family? What if we could be one?"

"I don't understand," she said.

Maybe it didn't make sense and he couldn't tell, because he didn't know how to do this. Because he wasn't as accomplished with human connection as he was at anything else.

"This marriage. What if we made it real?"

CHAPTER ELEVEN

WHEN VERITY HAD woken up this morning, she'd had to force herself to be angry. She had felt like her pride necessitated that she find a little bit of outrage and aim it at him, rather than letting him see that she was physically sated and ready to crawl in his lap and purr like a kitten.

So she had brought up the indignity of it all. Had tapped into the anger that had brought her into his bed in the first place last night. But he had met it with vulnerability, and that was something she didn't have a defense against.

Then he'd kissed her, and all of her anger had dissolved into a lavender haze. His touch, the things he said to her, the things he demanded of her, it was like he had reached into her and taken the golden threads of her deepest fantasies and spun them into a glorious reality.

He seemed to know her body better than she did.

And now *this*.

He was asking her for a real marriage, when they were both still breathing hard from the pleasure they'd found together. When she was still dizzy with her need for him.

"A real marriage?"

"Yes. It was a business arrangement before we slept together."

She wanted to get huffy about that. She wanted to minimize the meaning of what had happened between them the night before. Just like she had tried to do when he had brought up her virginity. She didn't want to be vulnerable about it; she didn't want to lend any credence to the idea that...that it had mattered that he was the first one.

But the truth was, it did.

And the truth was, it had changed everything to sleep with him.

Even if she didn't want to admit it. In fact, it didn't matter if she admitted it or not; he could clearly see it. Even Alex could see it.

He had told her things about himself. Not just the facts of his upbringing, but the way it made him feel. The image of him as a little boy in a classroom with other five-year-olds, realizing that they all went home to the same mom and dad every night, while his circumstances changed with the whims of the system, was truly heartbreaking. She couldn't hold her outrage as tightly as she wanted to with that picture in her mind.

But a real marriage...

She tried to drum up some of the horror she usually felt when she thought of marriage. A family. Of quiet suburban desperation.

But, Alex was not suburban. He could no more live on a cul-de-sac than he could fly to the moon. Actually, he was way more likely to fly to the moon. He was a billionaire after all, and space travel was accessible to him. Normality? Not so much.

So right there and then, she didn't need to worry about that. The image of life with him was... Well, it was different. Different than the generic imaginings she'd had of married life, whenever she had taken the time to think of them.

And maybe some of it was that she'd already lived through the wedding. Her family was there, and there hadn't even been a large explosion, even though she had felt like she was tearing herself into pieces to prevent it from happening.

So one of the worst parts of marriage had already been dealt with.

Are you insane?

Maybe. Maybe not. What was the alternative? The alternative was the two of them separating in six months like this had never happened. Her going on to live that independent life she had always thought she wanted.

Flashes of last night, of what had just happened, made her heart beat faster, made her body feel weak. She was just going to walk away from him when all this was done and never feel...this again?

"Six months," she said.

"What?"

"We make the decision in six months. Just like we were going to do, as far as how well the marriage was working externally. Only we'll be evaluating how well it's working...internally." She blinked, and noticed how scratchy her eyes felt. "I don't really know myself," she said. "It comes back to that protection thing. And I'm willing to entertain the idea of my life looking differently than I thought it would. But you're not wildly in love with me. That's not why you're suggesting we stay together."

"You're not wildly in love with me either."

Her comment and his returned volley were like arrows, whizzing by, but not hitting the target. Dangerous, somehow, even without contact. Certainly not an arrow she was willing to jump in front of, not now.

"No. But that isn't what we're talking about, is it? You hired me because you wanted a taste of the state that you don't know how to have. You wanted a sample of friendship. And I gave it to you. Now you want to see what it would be like to have a family. I know what it's like to have a family, and for me, it isn't happy or warm. Between us, maybe the potential is there. But that's all we are talking about. We are talking about making plans, laying out our terms, we're not talking about jumping headlong into an affair."

"You can say that after what happened last night?"

"Is that why you're asking me to stay married to you? You want more sex? What if I would have sex with you no matter what?"

She already knew that she would. She already knew that she didn't possess the self-control to stay away from him. Even if it would be smarter. Even if it would be the more prudent thing to do.

"I would still want more."

"Why?"

It was almost like she had reached out and grabbed him by the throat. He looked stricken. He looked like he didn't know the answer, and she realized right then that she had never seen Alex looking uncertain. Perhaps he had been at different times, but not so she could tell.

"Because when I think about what's on the other side of this, I no longer find pure satisfaction in the idea of simply achieving greater financial success. I... I tricked myself into thinking that's what I was looking for. It's not what I'm looking for. There is something missing from me. Something missing from my life, from my future. I cannot buy it, Verity, and you have no idea how much that...how much that burns. Because I never wanted to be helpless, not again. You make me feel more connected with a part of myself that I have never...that I have never touched before. Perhaps we are *friends*."

Friends.

Now, after he'd been inside of her, they were friends.

He had done it. Stuck the knife right between her ribs. Gotten her right where she was vulnerable.

The truth was, if he had tried to profess wild and sudden love for her she never would've believed him. She would've laughed at him; she would have said that he was manipulating her.

Friendship, though, and the chance to suit his soul, that was appealing in a way that she couldn't quite articulate. It appealed to the loneliness in her. Maybe that was why this made sense to them both. They were both essentially quite lonely—wasn't that obvious? She had taken a job that included surrendering her lunch hour to her boss. You only did that when you had no one else to take the hour with. So maybe this wasn't about love.

Maybe it was just chemistry mixed with the deep desire for both of them to not feel quite so alone. She had dedicated her life to protecting herself. But that protection had only built a wall around her that had left her isolated. Maybe this was a chance to knock that down.

"Six months," she said. "We can see how we both feel about it then."

"And you will live with me as my wife until then?"

"Yes. Though I think we need to define that."

"Forsaking all others. Giving yourself to me."

"Yes," she said. "You have to do the same."

"Easily done."

Whatever past affairs he'd had they were virtually invisible. If he was a playboy, he certainly didn't flaunt it, and so it was easy enough to believe him now. She would ask him about that someday. What his first time was like. How he treated sex, and lovers and all of that. She needed to ask him so many things. Because they didn't really know each other.

They sort of did. There was a veneer of knowledge that was a very good veneer, but it was a veneer nonetheless. It didn't go deep.

They had started to talk about real things just recently. They were going to have to keep doing that.

"All the rules that we had when we…when we worked together, they can't be the rules anymore. Every topic has to be open for conversation. Otherwise we can't get to know each other."

He stared past her. "That seems reasonable."

"You don't like it, though."

"I don't like my past. But I have shared more of it with you than I ever have with anyone, and I will answer any questions that you have."

But he wouldn't freely share. Maybe it wasn't fair to expect him to simply…start talking about things that he had always kept guarded. She couldn't demand everything from him at once. Just like she couldn't demand everything from herself at once. She was going to have to spend the next six months not just getting to know him, but really getting to know herself.

They were both going to have to be vulnerable.

Some secret, romantic part of her had longed for this. That felt very dangerous. The urge to romanticize this. That she had met him, and this was inevitable, whatever both of them had planned about their lives. That they would be swept into something bigger than themselves, bigger than everything.

No. She had to be honest. As Alex had. He might understand this, he might even want it, but it wouldn't be the deep love connection that other people looked for in marriage. And maybe that would make it safer. They could have boundaries, and discussions; it would be like working together. Everyone would have clear roles, and they would talk about things, and it would be…

She imagined holding a baby. The image was visceral

and raw, and something that she had never let herself think about before.

When she had decided she didn't want family, she had included children in that.

But what if they could have a baby?

Part him, and part her.

A beautiful connection that maybe Alex would feel.

What if he didn't?

She would. She had two whole parents who didn't care that much about her. If her baby had one that loved her with everything, she would be doing much better than Verity. And Alex would try. She knew that much.

For a moment she had an image of Alex standing on the other side of a glass divider, looking in at herself and that baby. That was tragic. She hoped that wouldn't be their future. But all she knew was self-protection, avoiding things like this, avoiding wanting too much to keep herself safe. She couldn't plan all this out.

She couldn't see every possible outcome.

But maybe she could hope. Maybe that wouldn't be so bad.

"Is your family still here?"

"Wow. I don't know, because I didn't plan any of this. And you know I didn't look at my phone even one time between last night and now."

"Yes. My apologies. Also find out their whereabouts and send them on their way. Then you and I shall go on our honeymoon."

"Honeymoon? Where?"

"Wherever you would like to go, Verity. Because

this marriage was once about me, my company and what you would get when it ended. But now it's about us. And so I want you to be happy. I want you to want to be with me."

She had the briefest notion that this was all too good to be true. But she and Alex had already lived lives that seemed a little bit too tragic to not be exaggerated. So why couldn't they have this instead?

This was a big step, a frightening one.

But the alternative was to go back.

And somehow, after everything, she knew that was impossible.

So she had to keep going forward.

Maybe this would be the key to finding herself.

Maybe she could fix him.

CHAPTER TWELVE

SHE HAD AGREED. All he knew was triumph. From the moment she said yes, to the moment his plane touched down on the private Caribbean island where they would be spending their honeymoon.

He had bought it some years earlier, but had never been, and it felt like the perfect place to try and become something different.

And she responded to the beauty of the location just as he hoped. As they disembarked from the plane, and she looked around at the smooth, crystal blue water, the white sand and bright pink flowers dotting the bushes, her face lit up with joy.

The over-water villa had been stocked in preparation for their stay and as they walked out on the gangway that took them to their accommodation, it wasn't the view that captivated him most. It was her.

The opportunity to give this to her. To watch her face as she took in each detail around them.

As she smiled when the breeze blew through her hair, the way her mouth dropped when he opened up the front door to the villa, and revealed an expansive living area with a vaulted ceiling. There was a small kitchen area with glossy black countertops and a bowl of fruit placed at the center.

And she was enraptured by all of it. "This is the most beautiful place I've ever seen," she said, taking a turn around the room, and then moving into the bedroom, before coming back out. "And this is the biggest bed I've ever seen."

Her cheeks turned instantly pink.

"Good for our purposes," he said.

He went into the kitchen area and opened up the fridge, where he found wrapped trays with precut fruit, a bottle of champagne and a tray of meat and cheese.

He began to get all of it out, taking down glasses and pouring a measure in his and hers.

"Why don't you go out to the deck. There should be appropriate clothing for you in the bedroom."

She looked at him with intrigue, then vanished back into the bedroom. He took his time preparing the trays, walking out to the expansive deck area and going to the loungers just outside the bedroom. He set the trays of food and champagne flutes on a table between two of the loungers, and then Verity appeared, wearing...

Nothing.

He thought his heart might beat itself through his chest.

"There are some beautiful things in there," she said. "But I did sort of think that since it's a private island..."

"I very much like the way you think."

She smiled at him and sat down in the lounger.

This, he knew, was a tease, because she was going to drink her champagne and have her snack. And he wanted her to be happy.

He was hard, though, and it made it difficult to focus on the food.

"This is really beautiful."

"I know," he said, never taking his eyes off her.

"Have you ever done anything like this before? I mean, with anyone else."

"No," he said. He looked at her. "Do you actually want to hear about past lovers?"

"No and yes. I'm curious how much of this is...a routine for you."

"None of it," he said, honestly. "I told you, I can have sex without romance. I do it all the time."

"How much is all the time?"

"Don't ask questions you don't want the answer to, Cricket."

"Ah. I am Cricket again."

"Does that bother you?"

"No. I like it. Because it's something that only you call me. But I also like it when you call me by my name. Because you never did, so when you started it felt like something. Special. Maybe that's why I'm asking you these questions. This feels special. I want to believe that it is."

"You're the only woman I've ever married. I wasn't protecting myself, not the way that you were. I wasn't afraid of accidentally getting attached to somebody that I didn't want to be attached to, or getting hurt by someone. I never have been. The first time I had sex was one of the most truly disappointing experiences of my life."

"Why?" She sat up, naked and holding a champagne flute, and it distracted him from the disturbing feelings that were rising up inside of him.

"I thought... I thought I might feel something. You're supposed to. The first time, it's supposed to mean something. It's supposed to matter. I didn't feel anything. If anything I felt more alone then than I ever had before. Like I was lying next to a stranger, and also like I was one." He tried to smile. "I suppose that's how it is when you sleep with a stranger. It feels like exactly what it is."

"How old were you?"

"Twenty-one. I didn't ever sleep with a woman until I had somewhere nice to take her. So not until I had some money. So that I could take her to a nice hotel. I dressed it up as something that looked like romance, and I thought perhaps I would feel it. I didn't. That was the day I knew that I was truly broken. I said goodbye to her, and I can't even remember her face now, all these years later. I couldn't remember her face very soon after, if I'm honest."

She got off the lounger, and moved onto his, scooting right next to him, then wrapped her arms around him, the gesture so unusual, so foreign to him, that he almost didn't know what she was doing. Hugging him. She was giving him a hug.

"That's very sad," she whispered. "And I'm sorry."

"Are you hugging me?"

"Yes. Because someone should."

Someone should. Was that true? Did he deserve those things, those simple gestures, connections, when he didn't know how to give them back? Or maybe what she meant was that he should've had them in the beginning, because then maybe he wouldn't be the way he was now. That he could see.

"To answer your question," he said, because he didn't know how to continue the conversation about hugging, "no. I have never brought anyone to a place like this. I've never spent time with a lover before. I've never had a relationship. And I suspect that's what this is."

"Is it?" She turned her head, rubbing her nose against his neck.

"I suspect."

"You're so funny, Alex."

"Not on purpose."

"I know."

They sat like that for a long time. It was an incredible thing, to want her, but to also be able to sit with her. In silence or otherwise.

"I think," she whispered finally, "you might be protecting yourself more than you know."

"In what way?"

"Never trying to have relationships."

"Why would I try something I felt I would inevitably fail?"

"You're trying with me."

It was true. He was. Except… She understood. She understood that he might not be able to…give what most men could.

"You know, though," he said, suddenly desperate to hear her say it. "You know who I am. You know how I am. You know that I might not be able to give you something that feels like...what every other relationship feels like."

"I don't know what any other relationship feels like. So I guess that's a good thing, isn't it? I don't know what it feels like to be with someone else. And I never wanted to be, not before you. When I said that I didn't know myself, what I meant was...admitting to myself that you were the one I wanted was a shock."

"What?"

"I never wanted Stavros. He was safe. I made rules for myself. Before I went off to school, I told myself I would never get involved with a man who would make me lose my head. I never wanted anyone who was intense, someone that I felt like I needed to manage them, or... You know how my family is. So I told myself that if I was going to date, it was going to be someone that I could manage. Then I took a job working for you, and you were definitely not someone that I could manage. Stavros being in the same building was convenient. He's handsome, he's not demanding. He smiles all the time. I could distract myself looking at him, and fill that surface need to be distracted by someone. So that I didn't have to admit I wanted you."

"You wanted me?"

"Yes. From the very beginning. That's also why it took me two years to ask Stavros out. I didn't really want to go out with him. I didn't really want him. I had gotten to the point where I thought maybe I was going to just have to do it, and maybe I would have. But somehow I doubt it. Being with you... I didn't even have to think about it. I didn't have to question it. It was right. It was what I wanted. That's why I'm here. It's easy for me to say that you railroaded me into this. Comfortable, even." She smiled. "But I'm not really being tortured, am I?"

"You might feel differently after several days in my company."

She laughed. "Maybe. Maybe. I'm trying to figure out all the things I've been ignoring. All the things I've been pushing down. You definitely taught me something about myself when we..."

"You like it when I praise you."

"Yes. I guess it doesn't take a psychologist to figure out why. I spent a long time feeling like I wasn't enough. Not good enough, not smart enough, not anything enough. That's one reason I enjoyed working for you so much. Because you are such a pain. You are so exacting, all the things that other people don't like about you I—" She stopped talking. "Sorry. I guess I shouldn't say it like that."

"It doesn't hurt my feelings that people don't like me. I've never tried to make them like me."

And there he wondered if she had spoken some wisdom to him a few moments ago.

He had never tried to make anyone like him. He had never tried to have a relationship. What if that was a version of self-protection?

No. He had wanted to feel something. There were times in his life when he'd wanted it desperately. But the feelings had never been there. It would be a convenient fantasy to tell himself that it had been self-protection all along. It would make him feel better, in some ways. But it would give both of them false hope.

"And then you had to. For work."

"Yes. I have always seen my company as my legacy. I always thought that I would never have children, and so it would have to be what remained of me. Do you understand?"

She nodded slowly. "And what do you think of children now? Hypothetically. If we were to stay married."

The idea fascinated and terrified him. Made him feel like he was on the edge of a cliff, and also on the edge of a brilliant discovery. A child. His child. A great and terrible experiment, he thought. Maybe the only chance he would ever have to love someone or something instantly and in an all-consuming way, but if he couldn't...

"Don't try to figure out if you'll be good at it. Just... Do you want a child?"

He nodded slowly. "Yes. I do."

"Me too. I didn't think I did, but thinking about it now it makes me realize that I do. But I want to build a family on my own terms. Can you imagine that? The power in finally taking control. You can have a family, and it doesn't depend on choices other people made. I can have a family, one that's as good as I make it.

Choosing to avoid this, it was always giving our power away. I realize that now."

When she said it like that it made sense. It was giving their power away. And neither of them would do that, not anymore.

"Finish your champagne. I need you."

"Oh. I'm finished."

Then he swept her into his arms and carried her to that big bed, and showed her exactly why they needed all that room.

CHAPTER THIRTEEN

AFTER TWO WEEKS on the island, Verity had forgotten who she was away from it. It was a blissful respite from reality that she had never really imagined taking before. And it was amazing. All they had done for two weeks was eat, make love, swim in the ocean and make love again. Sometimes she cooked food for him; sometimes he did it for her. They dined on the beach, on the deck outside of their bedroom, in bed.

If their lives could be like this, always, then everything would be okay. She was certain of that.

It was just too bad that away from here they had lives. Though, they got along so well in their professional lives. Maybe she could keep on being his assistant, even though she was his wife.

But this was only two weeks into the six months. She wasn't supposed to be making decisions about the future this early. Of course, they had talked about the future. About children.

Part of her wanted to throw caution to the wind and her birth control pills into the trash and tell him she wanted everything right now.

But she had a feeling that her desperation was more of her instinct to protect herself. To make this permanent. Because at this point, she was terrified of what it would look like if she lost him.

She was also struck by the difference between managing someone, and doing things for them because she wanted to. She had thought that a relationship would be labor. Work.

She and Alex did things for each other, and it made her happy. Cooking for him delighted her, because he enjoyed it. And she had never really gotten to take care of another person before. There was something lovely about it. Something deeply satisfying.

One night over dinner she realized that she didn't know one of the most basic things about him.

"When is your birthday?"

"Why?" he asked, looking deeply suspicious of her.

"Because I want to know what your astrological sign is so I can do our chart."

"You must be joking."

"I think you're a Taurus. But I am joking."

"I don't know what that means, but... I don't know exactly."

"What do you mean you don't know exactly?"

"I don't have a birth certificate from when I was actually born. I had one that the state filled out, but they can only approximate my age. I have never celebrated it on a specific day. It's in April. At least, that is their best guess."

"A Taurus. Most likely." She said that, and tried to

smile, but mostly what he had just said hurt. It hurt badly, because he didn't even know this most...basic thing about himself. She wished that she didn't know who his parents were, because she wanted to go and fight them. She wanted to go and fight a state that had made him feel useless, made him feel like his failure to be adopted was his fault.

She wanted to bake him a birthday cake and celebrate him and give him everything that he had ever been denied.

"It's never meant anything to me. My understanding is that those things only matter when you have someone to celebrate with."

"I don't know. I like my birthday just fine, even with the family that I have."

"I've never celebrated."

She decided that wasn't acceptable. She called their supply source and arranged for some gifts to be brought to the island, along with decorations and supplies for a recipe she'd been wanting to try for a while.

And then there was the cake. She was the most excited about the cake. Of course, with their situation on the island it wasn't exactly like she could surprise him. And anyway, she wasn't sure surprising Alex was the best thing to do with him. What she surprised him with, were the supplies.

"What is all this?" he asked as he helped arrange everything in the kitchen.

"I've decided that you're going to have a birthday party. I'm going to bake you a cake."

"It's not my birthday."

"I don't care. You've missed too many celebrations. And I'm going to celebrate you, dammit."

He looked at her like she was something strange and foreign, and maybe even wondrous. She couldn't deny that it made her feel a shimmering, pleasurable sensation.

She wanted him to say that he was happy with her. That the idea was wonderful. He didn't say that, but he didn't tell her not to do it. He hung out on the periphery of the kitchen area like an animal that had been banished, prowling like he was waiting for something.

"What are you cooking?" he asked over the invisible line that he had drawn for himself.

"Homemade pasta and scallops."

His eyes went sharp, and she recognized that he was pleased with that answer. Even though he didn't say, she was warmed.

He went back to pacing.

When she started hanging streamers around the room, his expression shifted to one of total shock.

"What?" she asked. "You can't have a party without streamers."

"I... I didn't know that."

"Well, now you do. It's festive."

There was something strange about the way he behaved after that. It reminded her the most of the way he was during work. That wall in place, like he was trying to observe some sort of custom very carefully. It was definitely not how he'd been acting during their time here. But she was determined to persist even though he was being weird.

Of course he was, if she really thought about it. He wasn't used to anything like this. He had said so himself.

The Happy Birthday that she wrote on the cake was a little bit lopsided, but she was pleased with it all the same. It was chocolate, and it would taste good, so it didn't really matter if it was pretty.

She put a candle in the center, ready for her to light once they were done with dinner.

"Go sit down outside, and I'll serve you."

He did what she said, but his movements were robotic.

And when she served him, he didn't get any warmer. She sat across from him, hoping to draw him out. He was stilted, but not unkind.

"I didn't even make you eat salad," she said, and that coaxed a small smile from him.

When they finished with dinner she went into the kitchen, lit the candle on the cake and brought it out to him. She sang, even if badly, and set the cake down in front of him. "And now you blow out the candle and make a wish."

He blew the candle out, and looked up at her with haunted, hollow eyes. And then he stood up, and walked over to the railing of the deck, resting his forearms against the top of it, staring out sightlessly at the dark water.

"Alex," she said. "What's wrong?"

"It doesn't mean anything to me," he said, his voice rough. "I don't...care about this."

The first thing she felt was pity. An enormous heaping of self-pity, actually, not pity for him. She had worked so hard on this, and he didn't care. It meant nothing to him that she had put all this effort in, that she had thought of him, that she had wanted to give him something that he had never had before. It meant absolutely nothing.

And then, just as suddenly as that welled up inside of her, it went away. Because of course that wasn't what he was saying. He wasn't saying that it didn't matter that she had done this; it was the party itself. It was his first birthday party, and he didn't know what to feel.

Because he didn't understand this. He had already explained how Christmas was for him. That he couldn't feel this thing he was certain he was supposed to because he had no nostalgia attached to it. Even worse, she suspected he had a host of pain associated with these things. Whether he wanted to admit it or not. Whether he even knew it or not. He had missed a lifetime of this.

And this was his deepest fear. She hadn't even thought of that. Hadn't considered it.

"Maybe it doesn't this time," she said. "But it can. This is just the first one. But next year, you'll remember this."

His face was half in shadows, his eyes black. "Why would I ever want to remember this? This reminder of everything that I'm not. Everything that I can't be."

"Then..." She felt like she was bleeding from the

inside. She felt like she had caused him pain when that was the last thing she wanted to do. And all she wanted to do was fix it. She just wanted to fix it. "Then let's make this the memory."

She kissed him. With everything she had. Kissed him with everything she had tried to put into the birthday party. Kissed him with all the desire inside of her. To be good for him. To be perfect for him.

To gain his praise, but now more than that. To make him feel. She wanted it. So much. So badly. To be the one who could change this. Who could change him.

He wrapped his arms around her, and kissed her back, his desperation matching hers. "I need you," she whispered. "I want you." She wanted to find the words. To find something to make him feel even half for her what she did for him. He knew exactly what to say to her. She didn't have the words for him.

"I need you," she said. Because it was true. Because it was the only thing she could think of.

He didn't carry her inside. Rather he picked her up and carried her over to the lounger, stripping her of her party dress and growling when she was naked beneath the moonlight. This wasn't that sweet gesture she was trying to offer him. This was something else. Something intense. Something feral. But this was what he needed, and she was going to give it to him.

Even if it cost her.

Intense. She had always sought to avoid intensity. She had wanted to go through life without connections that cost her.

That was her mistake.

This was so much better than being protected.

This was so much better than being safe.

She wanted him. Everything that he was. Everything. Even the broken things, the frightening things. The things that could wound her. After all, the way he was hurt him. Why wouldn't it hurt her sometimes? And the way she was... She had hurt herself with it. She had spent all this time denying herself. Hiding.

She wasn't afraid, not anymore. Maybe Alex would end up hurting her.

But he was worth it. He was so infinitely worth it.

That was the difference. The difference between him and her parents. The difference between everything that they could be, and everything that her family had been.

She chose Alex. And that was different in and of itself.

But more than that, he gave to her too. He had, over the years that she had known him, and he had while they had been here on the island. He took care of her. He gave her the words that she needed. Maybe he was best at all of it when they were in bed, but that was just the way he found it easiest.

He gave her something that made her feel good. He cared about making her feel good. This wasn't a one-way street. This was caring. Whether he knew it or not. She wanted him to understand that. This was connection. Maybe it was the only place he could feel it. Maybe. But then she would be here for him this way.

"I'm yours," she whispered. "You don't have to do

anything to try and keep me. I'm already here. I married you. You're my husband. I'm yours."

He shivered beneath her touch, and she maneuvered herself that she was straddling him on the lounger, unbuttoned his shirt as she felt him growing hard between her thighs. She kissed him. "I belong to you."

He reached up and gripped the back of her hair, pulling hard. The noise that he made was savage, and she kissed him, swallowing the end of it, claiming it for herself.

He wanted that. He wanted her. He wanted that connection that he didn't think he could feel. He wanted some external marker. Some form of proof. Her word. Her promise. She would give it to him. Because she cared for him. She cared for him so much.

She...

She pushed that thought away. She kissed him. Deeper, harder. Making a physical vow out of what she had already spoken.

Naked in the moonlight, she straddled him as she undid the closure on his pants and freed him so that she could position herself over him, take him inside, moving up and down slowly, luxuriating in the feel of him inside of her. The feel of this connection. "You don't feel nothing with me," she whispered.

She wasn't even sure if he could understand her. She wasn't sure if she was coherent.

But she knew that much was true. She wasn't some stranger that he lost his virginity to; she wasn't a birthday party.

He felt something for her. And he felt connected to her now. In this moment, they were something. In this moment, they were real.

She pushed them both to the brink, until he was shaking, sweating. Until a horrible, hollow-eyed look was gone, and it was replaced with need. Desire.

He was hers. She was his. This was true. Undeniably.

Even if he had a hard time admitting it. Even if right now he couldn't understand it.

He gripped her hips and took the control from her, thrusting up inside of her, his strength, the ruthlessness of each thrust driving her closer to the edge.

And when they fell, they fell together, even connected in this. In pleasure.

She lay down over him, her hair spread out over his chest like a blanket.

"You felt something then," she said.

He wrapped his arm around her, but said nothing.

Still. She knew that it was true.

She had to believe that it was true.

CHAPTER FOURTEEN

Alex didn't appreciate work intruding on their honeymoon. The reports that he was getting back were all positive; everyone who had an opinion on such things was fascinated by his marriage. Some thought it was a PR move, but many thought it was a romance novel come to life. A workplace romance between the beautiful and warm heroine and the hard remote hero. But one thing was becoming abundantly clear: his time away from work was beginning to be a bit too much, and he and Verity were needed back in the real world.

He found himself reluctant to leave, which was a strange feeling. Normally, his drive to work was the strongest drive he possessed.

But he found he wanted to stay here.

All the more reason to go, he supposed.

He took a breath, and walked through the kitchen area, deliberately not thinking about the failed birthday party from a week ago, through his shared bedroom with Verity, where she was not, and then outside. He looked down, and saw her in the clear water, swimming like a mermaid with her blond hair streaming behind her.

"Wife," he said, the word catching in his throat. "I need to speak to you."

She swam over to where he was, looking up at him, her smile in pitch. "I'm afraid we have go back."

"Oh," she said, looking disappointed. He hated that he had disappointed her. He hated that he had made her frown.

He had never cared how he made another person feel before. It was the strangest thing. Sometimes watching Verity was like watching a piece of himself out in the world. He could not explain it. Like she had taken something essential from him, stolen it and repurposed it. He wasn't even certain if he wanted it back.

"We must. While the headlines about our marriage have been positive, ahead of the product launch we need to be seen."

"Of course," she said.

"And so, we will be," he said.

A few hours later they were on the private plane headed back to Athens. "You said you wanted to go to London," he said.

"Well, yes, I would like that."

"Then we shall go. As part of all of this."

She tilted her head to the side. "Oh right. Just for show."

"We just had an entire honeymoon that had nothing to do with the outside world."

"I know. But it's hard to forget that this is actually

why we got married in the first place." She sighed. "Actually, it was really easy to forget. For a while. And now...reality is kind of lurching up to bite us in the face."

"Is that how you feel?"

She lifted her hand and made a claw with it. "Yes."

"Reality doesn't have to be a bad thing."

"In my experience, it is."

"Ah yes. Because in reality, it is not a fairy-tale wedding, it is a secret ambush by your family."

"Well. Yes. Not trying to be rude or whiny about that or anything, but that was a little bit rough."

"I had thought that we were past that."

"We are. Intermittently. Sometimes, I get a little bit mad about it, though."

"Well, I will tell you what I have planned. We must be seen tonight going back to our home in Athens."

She blinked. "I didn't move out of my apartment yet."

"Yes, you have. I took care of everything while we were on the island."

Her eyes nearly bugged out of her head. "You have had all my things moved?"

"Yes," he said. "It was a mere detail that needed to be seen to."

"Right. My entire life was a mere detail."

"That little apartment was not your entire life."

"I guess not." She looked irritated.

"Are you going to sulk, or are you going to tell me why you're being difficult?"

"What we had was really special. And now we're

going back to life. We're going back to work. It can work, I know it can. But I'm worried."

"Verity, I cannot promise you that I'll be a perfect husband in the way that the world would define it. But I'm not leaving everything that we were behind on that island."

He didn't know what else to say.

She seemed mollified by that. She looked almost happy.

"Well, I guess I can live with that."

"I would hope so."

"What is your plan then?"

"My plan is for us to be seen returning home tonight. Tomorrow we will fly out to London, we will stay in my town house there. Then we will go to dinner. I will take you off to Paris afterward, where we will swan romantically around the museums."

"Right. For everyone else."

"Also for us. Will you not enjoy it?"

"I will," she said. "I will. I'm determined to."

Though she didn't sound pleased in any fashion. "Good," he said.

When the plane touched down in Athens, he could feel her tension rising.

It was a short trip from the airfield back to his house, and he watched her face closely as they walked inside the ornate living quarters. Classical architecture mixed with modern design. If she was impressed, that wasn't what she was conveying. Rather she seemed perplexed.

"What is the matter?"

"I feel like a commoner going to live in a palace, I guess. I feel like... Okay, I don't actually care about that. I don't know how to live with another person. All of my things are here. With your things. We are going to share a bedroom. A life. It was different when we were in a neutral place, but this is your house. Your house, and here I am in it. And what do I even...? What you might even do to take up even a corner of a place like this? I worked really hard to become myself and I..."

"You're afraid of losing yourself," he said.

Because of course she was. She had shrunk herself, made herself small and insignificant in order to please her family. And now she was staring down watching herself melt into his world.

"I do not wish for you to become someone else. I don't need you to. I am strong enough to stand on my own feet, Verity, and I would think you would know that. Little Cricket, I want you to be my conscience. I want you to tell me what you need. And I want you to make your presence known. I always have. I did not hire you to sit there sight unseen. But you know that."

"But you don't feel attachment for anything. Or anyone. So what's to keep me rooted to this place? What's to keep you from replacing me? Or worse, me trying to reshape myself into something easier?"

He couldn't really argue with the thesis of that question. And yet, he didn't know for sure if he could say that he wasn't attached to her. For a moment, he let that thought sit there, marinate, grow in weight.

"It is not so simple. I want you with me. I know that much."

She softened. "Okay. Then I'll stay with you." She let out a long, hard sigh. "I'm sorry. You've been nothing but wonderful to me, all through our honeymoon together. You have never acted like you were a cruel man, and I've known you now for two years. But it's amazing how much weight parental issues carry. I know you didn't have them, but it's not…it's not different, not really."

"I know," he said. "I… I carry the issues of my childhood obviously. They have made me into who I am. And who I cannot be. For you or for anyone. But I have decided to vow myself to you. To make a family with you. Do you understand that's not something I would ever do lightly?"

"Yes," she whispered. "I understand that."

"Good. I'm glad that you do."

"It's so funny, because a few weeks ago it seemed reasonable to perform this for everybody. And now it feels a little bit too private."

"We will not show them everything."

"Of course."

Then, he picked her up off the floor, and swept her up the stairs, because he couldn't bear the weight of her uncertainty or sadness for another moment. He wasn't sure if that conversation had solved anything. Had made her feel any better. He wasn't entirely sure that he had gotten down to the heart of what was bothering her. But he cared about her. And he wanted her to be happy.

Or perhaps he only cared about himself and he wanted his home to be happy. Either way, he knew that talking wasn't the answer right now.

And when he laid her down in their bed, they didn't talk anymore.

And he felt everything he could not put into words.

The next morning they were off to London, and Verity was poring over the photographs of them entering their house in Greece.

"People really are...interested in us."

She had had a near breakdown last night, and she felt a little bit embarrassed by it now. Because it had been a full panic with very little articulation behind it. She supposed she should feel proud that she had been able to have it, and not worry so much about what he would do or think.

She had wanted him to say that he...that he cared about her. She had wanted something stronger than what she had gotten.

But if she wasn't willing to say...

She couldn't quite find it in her to put words to her feelings yet. And if she couldn't do that, then how could she expect him to do it? It wouldn't be fair.

She took a sharp breath, and looked at the photos. Looked at the two of them. She could see her bad mood, but it didn't seem like anyone else could.

She felt so exposed. They had been thrown from the gorgeous Caribbean and into a fishbowl. But that was the idea. This whole relationship was supposed to be for show. Acting upset about it now was pointless. Silly.

Childish, even.

Yes. It was childish.

She swallowed hard, trying to ignore the tenderness in the center of her chest. And trying to drum up some excitement for London.

"Yes, of course people are interested in us," he said. "Because I've never been attached to anyone before."

"I guess that's the thing. I should say that people are interested in you. They're only interested in me as an accessory."

"It is important. If you were a sort of corporate-looking woman, you wouldn't be right for the part."

The word *part* graded.

"Yes. Of course. It was a good casting decision. Going with kind of a bohemian hippie chick."

"I wouldn't call you that."

"Because you haven't really seen me in my own clothes."

He tilted his head, looked at her as if she had gone mad. "Of course I have. I've seen you at work every day for the last two years."

"Those are my work clothes."

"But then I saw you on our honeymoon."

"Mostly naked, and otherwise in clothes that were furnished by you. Or rather, your people."

"What do you normally wear?"

"Lots of bracelets, flowing skirts."

"I saw your family. They were aggressively…"

"Mid-level department store?"

"Well. Yes."

"When I was younger, I wanted to find some way to be an individual. To be me. Little things that were authentic, especially because I was always shoving pieces of myself down to make everybody else happy."

"I want to see them. I want to see that part of yourself."

His eyes glowed with the truth of that, and she felt so warmed by it. Renewed.

"Then, you will."

It was always nice when she found ways to talk to him. She could info dump on him, sure, the same way that he did her when they had gone over their pasts, but it was exciting to discover these kinds of things. These little things that they didn't know about each other yet, even though they have been so intimate with each other.

Even though she was finding new ways to touch him every day, there were still so many things to discover.

And every time he did, he seemed happy. He seemed to care. No one else in her life ever had.

When the plane touched down in London, the first thing they did was go to his town house. She realized that this was the opportunity she had missed when they had gone to Athens. She was busy feeling afraid. Because she had gone ahead and let herself get worried about what it meant for the two of them to be in the public eye. But here she was, in a house that had been put together especially for Alex. That meant that she could get to know him in a different way.

It was wild to her to think that she had married this man and she hadn't really been to his house.

She walked straight through the entryway, down the hall and into the kitchen. She went over to the stove and opened a cupboard just above it.

"What are you doing?"

"Looking for coffee. Tea. Little things about you. I haven't really snooped around one of your houses."

"We just stayed in my over-water villa."

"Well yes. But also no. Because you said yourself you hadn't even been there. You bought it sight unseen. It wasn't really yours."

"I rarely spend any time here."

"What do you like?"

"Coffee. Not tea."

"Okay. What else?"

"We have a dinner reservation, and you should get dressed."

"When is it?"

"Soon."

She fixed him with an irritated scowl. "Okay. Do I have enough time to go out and buy something for myself?"

"I... Why?"

"You said you wanted to see *me*. My taste. Who I am outside the office, who I was before I came here. I want you to know me."

"We don't have time tonight. And, also, this is for the cameras, it isn't for us."

She felt a little bit like she had had her hand slapped.

Like she had found her limit. She knew that it was a silly thing to be upset about, but she felt herself deflate. "Oh."

"Why are you looking at me like that?"

"You said you wanted to see my clothes. You said you wanted to see *me*. You don't, really. Do you?"

"I do. But tonight we are performing for the cameras. I will wear a suit and tie, regardless of what I might wear if we were on an island together."

"Right. Sorry. It's a silly thing. I'm being oversensitive. I feel like I've been oversensitive since we got back."

"Well. I didn't want to say anything."

She made a tsk-tsking sound, and went up the palatial staircase without asking him where his bedroom was. She had a feeling she could guess the whereabouts easily enough. He followed her, though.

"If you know you're oversensitive then why are you being oversensitive?"

She turned around, her head practically swiveled all the way around, in fact. He was standing in the doorway, looking maddeningly male, and she had the sudden blessed insight as to why she hadn't pursued relationships ever, in her whole life. Because this was the exact thing women complained about.

"I can't stop myself from having feelings. Moreover, very importantly, I won't. I have feelings, Alex. Having to leave the island like that, it was abrupt. I'm adjusting. I told you that this feels really personal."

"And I told you that I can't quite understand that."

"I'm sorry that you can't. But it's not going to make me feel any different. What the two of us have is intimate for me. I've never slept with anyone else. I've never... Alex, the relationship that I have with you is not like any other relationship I've ever had. I want to protect it. And I wanted to be mine. I want...to make you birthday cakes and be your wife. I don't want to perform it. It just reminds me that you didn't choose me. Not really. I'm part of the scheme."

"That's where you're wrong. I did choose you. I told you. Everyone likes you. There is something in you that draws people to you, and I don't even have a fraction of that. I'm brilliant," he said.

"And very modest," she pointed out.

"Honest," he said. "I'm brilliant at certain things. But I can't do the things that you do. The way that you make people feel is... You warm them up from the inside out, Verity. You even do it to me. You asked me...you asked me why I hired you. And I lied to you."

She froze. "You did?"

"Yes. I said that you were the first applicant. That wasn't true. I had interviewed several people at that point. Men, women. People closer to my own age. People with similar interests in technology. No one was you. There was something about you when you walked in, and I just knew that I couldn't let you walk back out. I knew that I had to have you. Every day. I knew that I needed you sitting across from me. I knew that you were the person that was going to teach me what I needed to know. And it couldn't have been just anyone.

That's why I wanted you to marry me. Because I knew that you would affect everyone the way that you do me. Because no one affects me. Nothing. Which means the board is going to love you—and they do. The public is going to love you."

It was very nearly the sweetest thing anyone had ever said to her. It was maybe the sweetest thing he'd ever said. But it wasn't altogether that sweet.

She had touched something in him, and he had immediately figured out how to make it useful.

She was awash in a strange sort of sentimentality, and also a fair amount of pain. Because it was just the most Alex. She meant something to him, and so he had figured out a way to make it relevant to his business.

Maybe she should just be happy that she meant something to him.

"Sorry. I will let you get dressed."

"Yes. Thank you."

She went to the closet, and fished out the most flowy dress she could find. Amazing how he had brought a whole wardrobe here too. She frowned as she touched the dress. These were the things that he saw her in. Because he knew her at the office. She fought off an intense wave of sadness. Fought off the terrible impression that in some ways, she was just still his assistant; it was just now it was for better or worse until death, rather than until HR separated them.

She had the jarring realization as soon as she finished getting dressed that this wasn't even permanent.

She really had lost all sense of everything on that island. She had lost all sense of self-preservation—that was for sure. She was in the deep end. She was also acting like he had all the control. When in fact, she could choose to walk away just as easily as he could choose to boot her back out into obscurity.

That should be cheering. It wasn't.

She took a deep breath, and walked out the door, coming face-to-face with him. And right then, she realized something. "I'm sorry," she said.

"You're sorry?"

"Yes. I'm acting... I'm being... It's fine. The way I'm being is actually fine, because my feelings are actually fine. But I realize that I feel insecure about how well we know each other, and how well we don't. I don't know my parents. Not as human beings. I know them as these terrible people that inflicted so much damage on to me, but I have no idea how they turned into those people. And I had to build up so many walls to keep myself safe, that I think I'm just very aware of...walls."

"I do not wish to hurt you, but I'm...me. And that means the wall is somewhat inevitable. Especially right now. Because this is the business aspect of this arrangement. But I gave you the honeymoon."

She wished that he didn't make it sound so much like a forfeit.

"True. You did."

She decided to let it go, because now they had to go out. And she did feel a moment of radiant sun when he held her hand, and led her into the restaurant. She didn't know why she felt so raw about them being on display.

But she had to try and sort it out instead of just taking it out on him. No, she didn't want to get into a situation where she suppressed her feelings, but at this point, she was just whining at him.

You're being a coward, is what you're doing.

She shut that thought aside.

And she had a lovely dinner with her husband, and didn't let herself worry for the whole rest of the night.

CHAPTER FIFTEEN

THE HEADLINES WERE FANTASTIC, but his wife was prickly. And he didn't quite know what to do with her. So when they went to Paris the next day, he made a few calls. Yes, they would have to do some things that put them in front of the public, but he wanted…he wanted to give her something. Something he had never given to anyone before. Not that it was difficult. He had never given anything to anyone before. That was one of the astonishing things about Verity. Taking care of her was something glorious.

When they were in bed, he had an easy time praising her. Telling her how special she was, but he could see that it wasn't quite enough for her.

He could see that she was craving something more, and he wanted to find a way to give her that.

He wanted to give her everything. It was just he didn't know where everything extended inside of him. Where it began. Where it ended.

"I want to go shopping," he said.

She looked up at him from their lunch table, right at

the base of the Eiffel Tower. "You want me to...go shopping? For something that will look good in photographs?"

"Something that looks good to you. You have no budget. I have a few things to arrange, and then I will have you meet me back at our hotel."

"Very heavy-handed."

"Perhaps. But you're a good girl," he said. "And you will do as I say."

She flushed with pleasure, and he thought perhaps that he had done well.

Taking care of business was actual torture, when in fact he wanted to be with her. She kept sending him photographs from dressing rooms, and he didn't quite know what to do with it. She was asking his opinion, and he found himself more interested in the cut of flowy skirts than he had ever been before in his life.

He had thought that he would prefer the outfits that showed more skin, that were tighter, the sorts of things that she often wore to the office, or the shockingly pink dress that she had worn to dinner that night in Athens. He found that he could easily make a fantasy out of swirling, flowing fabric.

And all that wild blond hair.

He was on a video call, and it was his head of production that caught him being distracted. "Mr. Economides?"

"Sorry," he said. "My wife is texting me."

It was perhaps the most normal sentence he'd ever said in his life.

It made him feel something. The beginning of something warm, right there at the center of his chest. He put his hand there, and he tried to ignore the burning pain that accompanied it.

He tried to get his focus back on the meeting.

He was meeting her soon. He was quite literally counting down the minutes.

When at last he was free of his obligations, he raced to the front of the hotel, where she stood wearing a glorious, emerald green dress with a drop waist and glimmering gems all over it. She was wearing a large cuff on her wrist, and it made him think of how he wanted to grab her, hold her down, hold her to him. It was shockingly erotic, as was every detail. Including the long teardrop earrings that nearly kissed her shoulders. It was different to what he had seen her in before, except it did remind him just slightly of the wedding gown that she had selected. Something ethereal about it. Magical.

That same, painful feeling began to splinter at the center of his chest.

He swallowed hard. "Let's go."

He swept her into the back of the limousine that took them across the city to the Musée d'Orsay. He had rented it out for the night, only for the two of them.

"Isn't this closed?" she asked as they approached the ornate building.

"Yes. For everyone who isn't us. But tonight, you and I get to have a private tour."

A flush of pleasure overtook her face.

"Just us?"

"Yes."

"Not for show?"

"No," he said. "I just want to see your face."

It was true. He wanted to give her something. In this museum, which contained so many of the beautiful works of art in the world, that seemed like a small thing. Something lovely that he could make for the two of them. They walked inside, beneath the glorious arched roof. The garden of sculptures greeted them.

It was lit still, but there were not even security guards. He had paid handsomely for the privilege. And for all of the security cameras to be turned off.

Tonight, this place might as well be their own private bedroom.

It was their own world.

"Do you like museums?" she asked, circling the first sculpture with an expression of wonder on her face.

"I never have. Do you like it, though?"

"I do," she said. "How did you know that I would?"

"You're one of those rare people who finds the beauty in so many things. You've talked to me often about how you used to walk through the art museum at your university. You always go to the beach on your day off, even though it's a long drive, and it eats into your precious free time. You like the beauty of things. This outfit that you chose tonight…it reflects that. You're a sensual creature, and you love things that are beautiful just for the sake of it. And so a museum is the perfect place for you, I would think."

"Tell me again," she said. "Tell me again why you hired me."

"Because I couldn't let you go," he said.

There was a real, raw emotion behind those words, even if he couldn't quite untangle what it was.

He paused for a moment, and stopped with her in front of a sculpture of a young woman sitting down, a harp beside her. It was so real, like she might grab hold of the instrument and begin playing at any moment. But she was just marble. Like him. The notion was so funny, he nearly laughed.

He looked real. Sometimes, he even thought he might be. When he was with her. When he could feel her heart beating next to his. But it was just her.

It had been, from the beginning.

He had wanted to cling to it, wanted to grab onto it, not let it go. From the first.

It would be so easy to confuse it with his own humanity.

"You know," he said. "I used to tell myself that I was only the right visit away from having a real set of parents. And every time a couple would come and see me and leave without me, never call back, never seek me out again, I would tell myself that perhaps I had gotten close that time. Perhaps, I had been on the cusp of having a family, and it had been cruelly snatched away from me. And then one day, I was perhaps nine, I realized that I was never close. They came on a visit to see a child. That visit didn't mean they thought anything about me in particular. It only meant they wanted a boy of my age. Nothing was taken from me, because nothing was ever mine. Because it was all forms and paperwork and things like that. It was nothing real. It was never me. I let go of all of it. Of even the wish for a family."

"Were you ever angry?"

"Yes. But I realize, you don't do anything to be born into a family. You simply are. You don't ask to be created. God knows I didn't. But here I am. Here you are. You didn't ask for your parents, any more than I asked to not have any. I imagine there are a great many children who are terrible. Who hate their parents, despise them, and aren't grateful for a single moment they spend with them. It's a lottery of birth, isn't it? I didn't deserve my life any more than you deserved yours. So yes. I used to be very, very angry about that. But there's no point to it. No purpose. It's just easier for there to be nothing," he said.

"You did feel," she said. "You used to be attached."

"What? There was never anything there."

"There was, though. A woman gave birth to you. She carried you in her womb for nine months. Just because you didn't know her didn't mean that connection didn't exist."

"I don't even know if she ever held me."

His words were far too loud in the silence of the museum.

"She did, though. Even if it wasn't in her arms."

"So did your mother," he said.

"I can't deny that. And you know, you don't have to be grateful to her. I'm not grateful to my mother. It's still a loss, though. That potential. It's a connection.

And I think maybe it's even worse because it is, even if it was severed the moment she gave birth to you."

"No," he said. "Don't mistake me. If any part of me ever felt connection, it was gone a long time ago."

"It still does. Or you would've been happy enough to let me walk back out of your life the day that I walked in."

Her words were like a knife slipped beneath his skin. "Verity…"

"Let's walk," she said, taking his hand and moving him into another display room. The works of Monet were hung with only dark walls and spare lighting to highlight them. One painting in particular caught his eye. It was meant to be Parliament, but it was obscured. The shape of it was clear, but it was like there was a fog all around it. And yet again, he couldn't help but think of himself.

Only the shape of a man, obscured by too much to ever really be clear.

Perhaps this was why he didn't like museums.

There were too many opportunities to look at himself. And if he wanted to gaze into a mirror he could've stayed back at the hotel.

They entered the display room for van Gogh, and Verity exhaled a reverent breath. They might have stepped into a church.

The approached the *Starry Night* painting, her features softening, a small smile on her lips. "It's so beautiful in person, I had no idea."

He looked at it, at the strokes and color, the bright

and the dark. He didn't feel whatever Verity did. When he looked at her, though, he felt...

She closed her eyes.

"What are you doing?" he asked.

"Wishing," she said, looking up at him. "If you wish on a star, your dreams could come true."

She'd said that once, in his office more than a month ago. "I never do that."

"You try it."

"I have everything already." Those words felt hollow, though, until she touched him, leaning against his arm, and right then he had the sense they could be true.

He said nothing, and the two of them continued to walk through the museum, back around into the hall filled with sculpture.

He looked at her standing there. "You could be one of these works of art," he said. "Aphrodite."

Her cheeks went flushed. "I think you're flattering me."

He grabbed her chin. "When have I ever given you the impression that I care to flatter anyone? I don't. I never have." It was the deepest truth he had. She was beautiful. She belonged here. She belonged...with someone who really cared about her. She was precious and perfect and lovely. And it was like a wall stood between them, and he did not know how to scale it. A fog, a great mist. Or perhaps he was simply made of marble. That was the truth of it. It was easy to say she belonged in the museum because of her beauty, but he was the one frozen.

He could be locked away in here for the rest of time and stay the same.

He felt a clawing desperation, to make these thoughts go away. To feel something. Anything. The way he could only feel when he touched her.

"Beautiful," he said again. He leaned in and kissed her neck, and she shivered. "We are the only ones here," he said.

"I know," she whispered.

"There are no cameras. There are no guards."

"We can't," she said, a fierce spark in her eyes.

"We can."

He was beginning to realize something. And he didn't want to have the realization. What he wanted to have was her. At least one last time. "Let me," he whispered.

He reached around to the back of her dress, and unzipped it slowly, letting it fall around her. And she truly did become one of the glorious pieces of art, standing there with her blond hair wild around her shoulders, her breasts full and glorious, her waist nipped in, her hips round. That pale thatch of curls between her legs a glorious temptation.

This was the closest he would ever come. To feeling real. Because of her.

This was what he had known from the moment he had met her. That there was a power that she held to reach him. But he didn't have the power to take hold of her. He could keep her. Physically.

But he would never be able to...

He didn't want to think. For the first time in his life, he wanted to feel. Only.

He moved toward her, and kissed her on the lips. "Oh, Verity."

He lifted her up, and laid her down on one of the white stone benches, and she let her head fall back as she looked up. She did look just like one of those statues. Except she was real.

Except she was there. He could touch her. He could taste her. He could have her.

They were flesh and blood. For now.

It didn't matter he saw himself obscured in all of these art pieces. It didn't matter if outside of these walls he was nothing more than cold marble. Right now, with her, he was a life. Breathing.

Right now he could have her.

Right now.

He began to undress, leaving his clothes scattered on the floor along with hers. She looked up at him, a smile curving her lips. "You look like you're cut from stone."

He grabbed her hand and put it up against his stomach. Moved it up toward his chest.

"Oh, but no you're not," she whispered. She closed her eyes. "I can feel your heartbeat. So fast."

"Only for you," he said.

He had never been conscious of his heartbeat before. Only with her.

He kissed her, all the better to drown out his thoughts. But he could still hear his own heart raging in his ears.

Kissed her neck, down to her breasts.

And he poured all of his desire out onto her. He told her how beautiful she was. Because he never got tired of praising her.

In this, he understood what it was to have someone. For the first time.

Oh God, to have someone and to want to keep her forever.

No one had ever wanted him in that way. No one had ever held onto him. But maybe it was because they couldn't.

And maybe if you couldn't, the kindest thing to do was to let the person go.

Verity had been trapped. In a house full of people who cared for themselves and not for her. Here she was, free and beautiful and his, but what would the cost be to her? She had been unhappy from the moment they had gotten here. She didn't like having to perform. Obviously reminded her of living with her parents. Would he ever be able to be any different?

He had never wanted something for someone else more than he wanted something for himself, but he was feeling the deepest desire for it now. For her. To be happy. Even if it meant being away from him.

His first impulse had been to hold her forever. To hire her, to keep her with him.

It had been like that from the beginning. She had never only been an employee to him. Not even for a moment.

No. She had been special, from the very beginning. And he was…broken. He could hide it because of all the money he had made. Because of all the success that he had.

He had told her with such confidence he wasn't broken, but where was the evidence of that?

His bank account? What did it matter? It meant nothing. Anyone could have money. Anyone could lose it. Anyone could be born into a family or make a child. But connection. Love. That was the one thing that wasn't guaranteed to everyone. The one thing you couldn't create or manipulate or buy.

He had none of it. If it was possible, his money would have been sufficient.

But it wasn't. It wasn't.

And neither was he.

But he was too weak to let her go before he took her again. Surrounded by all this beauty.

He claimed her, he said goodbye to her, he kissed her, and he fought against the crumbling feeling at the center of his chest. Because there was no point. There was no point. He had to keep the wall because it served him. He didn't know how to let go of the wall because it kept him safe. And somewhere in there all of his thoughts became confused, because if he had to hang onto the wall then was it inevitable? Or could he knock it down, could he...?

No. No.

She arched against him, and he gave himself over to her as he felt her take her pleasure. He took his own. Clung to her until the last bit of pleasure had been wrung from him.

She sat up and touched his face. He closed his eyes.

"Let us get dressed," he said.

She looked concerned, and he knew why. He was already putting distance between the two of them.

She dressed, and the two of them walked out of the museum, where their car was waiting.

"That was...that was quite literally the wildest thing I have ever done, or considered doing. That was—"

"I can't talk about this," he said.

She frowned. "That was... It was good, right?"

She was talking about sex. And something was falling to pieces inside of him. Anger rose up inside of him, and he knew it wasn't fair. None of this was fair.

He texted instructions to the driver, who began to pull away from the curb.

"Where we going?"

"The airport."

"Why?"

"You're going back to Athens."

"I am?"

"Yes, Verity. You're going back to Athens. Because this... We cannot continue this. I'm sorry. I manipulated you into this, and I have been using you. I can't do it anymore. This is...this is a broken man's equivalent of trying to be a real boy, and I am not accomplishing it. I'm just hurting you."

"I don't understand. We just had the most beautiful evening. We just had... we just had sex on a bench in a museum. And now you're telling me that you're sending me away?"

"You've been unhappy since we came back from our honeymoon."

She froze for a moment, looking straight ahead. "I haven't been unhappy since we got back from the honeymoon. I've been freaking out. Because... It was so easy when we were in that little cocoon. And suddenly we came back here, and I realized that my feelings were different. It was easy to tell myself it was the honeymoon, but we came back to reality and they came with me. I'm sorry. I should've told you. I love you, Alex."

The words hit him with the force of a slap.

"You don't love me," he said. Those words, those words that had never been said to him before, being spoken so easily in the silence of a car moving through the prison streets, seemed grotesque. They seemed like a farce; they had to be. Because it could not be so easy. It couldn't be.

For someone to love him, after all these years. No one ever had.

No one ever had.

"I do. I love you and—"

"You loved Stavros two months ago."

"I didn't. I already explained that to you. He was a distraction. Because the minute that I walked into your office I was drawn to you. Why do you think I took the job? Why do you think I threw myself into being the best assistant to you? Why do you think I said yes when you told me that I was going to marry you?"

"I manipulated you. I manipulated the entire situation. I made it so you couldn't say no, and you made it very clear that I did that."

"As I'm fond of saying to you when I'm trying to be

a brat, I do have agency. And yes, I also like to avoid unpleasant situations, and I definitely didn't speak up for myself when I should have or could have. But I would've chosen to marry you either way. You deserved to be scolded for the way that you went about it, but I would have... I would have. Because...because I love you. I made all these rules for myself. Not to get involved with an intense man. Not to want a man that could hurt me. And I knew you were that man. From the moment I met you I knew you were that man. But that wasn't about there being something wrong with you. It was about there being fear in me."

"This isn't what I wanted."

"Then what did you want? You said you wanted to try this. What did you think it would be? What did you think marriage would look like? Did you honestly want me to never have any feelings for you? Did you think that was the key to happiness?"

"No. I didn't think. I just wanted to keep you trapped. I wanted to keep you mine. You're right, though. It has nothing to do with you." The lie tripped off his tongue, because he knew that it would keep him safe. Because he knew that it was exactly what he needed to push her away.

To keep the walls safe inside of him.

"What I wanted was for you to be that perfect version of yourself that you are when you're pleasing everybody. What I wanted was your trauma, Verity, because it helps cover mine. That has nothing to do with you. It isn't right for me to keep you with me."

He could tell that he had done it. That he had taken a verbal knife and stabbed it straight through her heart.

She took a deep breath. "Okay. I'm not going to debase myself for the privilege of more rejection. But I'm also not going to make this easy for you. Because if that's true, then you're everything you said. You're a liar, you're cold, you're heartless. But I don't think you are. I think what you are is a coward. Do you know how I know that? Because you said you didn't feel anything when I made you that dinner, when I made you a birthday cake, but I think you did. The way that you prowled around the kitchen like a hungry dog looking for scraps. You want it so much and it scares you. You're afraid to admit it. All of the stories that you've told me of the boy that you were don't make me think of a man with no feelings. No. You're just still that terrified boy. Waiting for someone to love you, and now that it's happening you don't know what to do. Even worse, I think you love me. I think it scares you."

"No," he said. "Because I don't know how to love, and I never have."

"I just think you don't know what it is. This terrible, awful, clawing feeling inside of you, that's love. It's uncomfortable. It pushes you, it challenges you. Love does not ask you to sit comfortably, it asks you to do things. To sacrifice. It isn't a warm, fuzzy feeling that makes you feel a sense of euphoria. It can be that, it has been that. When we're together and you tell me that I please you, it is that. When I can be perfect for you and you can be perfect for me, and we are naked, but that's the honeymoon. Then we have to bring it into the real world, and that's when it's hard. We have to confront the things about ourselves that aren't whole. And that's hard. You're going to have to change. That's hard. But that doesn't mean that it's wrong. It doesn't mean we aren't supposed to have this.

"I learned this from loving you. I know you can feel something," she said. "You're just going to have to risk your feelings. I think you have them. I think you have more than most people, not less. You just need to be brave enough to let yourself have them." She reached forward and knocked on the divider between them and the driver.

The divider went down. "Stop the car," she said.

"Verity? What are you doing?"

"I'm getting out. I'm not going back to Athens. I'm not going back to work with you, I'm not... Whatever you think is happening—"

"You aren't getting out here in the middle of the city."

"Yes, I will. I can. I don't care if you're mad at me." She took a deep breath. "I don't care if you're mad at me," she repeated. "You deserve to be uncomfortable. You'll have to figure out why. And I'm not going to make it easier for you. I'm going to make you do the hard work. Because I deserve that. Don't you understand? This, this thing we have, it's real. We didn't just take care of ourselves, we took care of each other. And it could be the most wonderful... It could be everything. If you would just let it."

She pushed open the car door and got out, stumbling

onto the street. He unbuckled and followed her. "You've lost it," he said.

"Who cares?" she shouted back, walking away from him.

"And you're making a scene."

"I don't care about that either. You can keep your money. You can keep everything. I always had a choice. And now I'm choosing myself. My self-respect, if nothing else. And I'm choosing to value what I feel. I'm not going to squish it down, squeeze it, contort it into something to make you feel better. I'm not. I have my own money saved up. And I can get another job. I walked away from a situation that didn't fit me before, and I made it out the other side. I'm going to keep doing it. I really wish... I really wish you would let yourself be happy someday, Alex. Even if it isn't with me." She turned away, and kept walking. Then she paused. "Just make sure you eat a salad every once in a while, please." She lifted her hand and wiped a tear away from her cheek, and kept on walking.

He wanted to go after her. But something stopped him.

The very thing that had told him to send her home in the first place.

It stopped him now; all he did was stand there.

Yes. He was a billionaire. With all this power.

Left frozen by a woman.

By that woman.

And he did not think he would ever be the same.

CHAPTER SIXTEEN

BY THE TIME she checked into the small hotel—which was a serious downgrade from where she had been with Alex, Verity felt crumpled and reduced.

The whole day had been an emotional roller coaster, and the end of it had been...everything she was afraid of, really.

Everything.

It was why she had been holding it back. That declaration of love. Because what good had it done to say it?

She wiped at the tears that kept on tracking down her cheeks. "Alex, you idiot."

He had taken her on the most romantic date. He had made love to her, and it was glorious like always. He had made her believe in something impossible, beautiful and glorious. And then he had gone into hiding again.

She supposed yelling at him had been character development for her. She hadn't felt the need to placate him either. How funny. His anger didn't scare her. Her own didn't either, not now.

However, it felt like a hollow victory. Maybe she wouldn't really feel like she had changed until she yelled at her parents like that. She thought about it. She thought about calling them and screaming at them, years' worth of pent-up rage. But the idea didn't... It didn't fill her with any kind of satisfaction.

Mostly because it wasn't what she wanted. She didn't get mad at Alex to satisfy something in herself. She had done it because she was desperate to reach him. There had been a purpose to it. There was no purpose talking to her parents. They wouldn't change. They hadn't. But she had. She would continue to change. She would keep on doing it, even without Alex. Even though...

Her life would be less without him. She had loved him from the first moment she had met him. Someday, maybe she would celebrate the risk she had taken. That she had taken steps to actually get to know herself rather than just protect herself. He had taught her a lot. About her own bravery. About her desires. About what mattered to her, and what wasn't negotiable in the end. So maybe she should just be happy. Someday. Not now. Now she would be miserable. She would eat pastries, and lament. She would sit in her feelings and feel them. Because she wasn't hiding from anyone. Not him, not herself.

They had both spent their whole lives being so afraid of discomfort. So afraid that it would never end. She had put on a happy face and tried to make everything around her nicer, more comfortable. He pretended he didn't feel. And she could see now that a lifetime of that created a bland life that contained no authenticity.

They had touched it with each other.

But she was ready to drown in it. He wasn't.

He had hired her to be his conscience. So she had to stand firm even now. Because letting him continue to lie to himself, letting herself live a lie, that would be against everything that was right.

She lay back on the bed, and tried to sleep. But the bed was too empty without him. So instead, she went to the window and looked out at the city below.

The city of love.

Well. She had risked everything for love here. Had incredible sex in a museum. It was an exceedingly Parisian thing to do.

As she sat staring at the Eiffel Tower lit up in the distance, and crying over her broken heart, she figured that was very Parisian of her too.

In the end, he had gone back to his hotel room in Paris, and hadn't come out for two days. He finally got a call from the board president telling him he needed to get back out there.

"I have no desire to. Not now. My wife and I are separating."

"You can't separate from your wife now," the man said, practically spluttering with outrage.

"Well, it's a shame, because I am. She has left me."

"You have to get her back. You have to pay for her to come back."

"It will fix nothing."

"It will fix the optics for the company. Your relationship with Verity Carmichael is the single best thing that has ever happened to you."

Those words echoed inside of him. Because he agreed. He agreed on every level.

Verity had been the single greatest thing that had ever happened to him, and in the end, he had to send her away. Because just looking at her…

He felt sick with regret. With helplessness.

It reminded him of being a boy. Passed around from home to home. Gawked at by potential parents but never taken home. He had always vowed he would never feel this way again. And she had made him. She had done this to him. She…

She had fundamentally changed something inside of him. He had lost control of himself. He had thought all of his life that he didn't have the ability to connect to another person, and she had shown him what that could be like. Just for a moment. And she was acting like he chose…like he chose to stay alone?

He had never chosen this. Not ever.

For the first time in your life someone reached out to you, someone said they wanted to be with you, and what did you do?

He growled.

"Mr. Economides," the president said, his voice placating. It brought Alex back to the moment.

"What is happening between myself and Verity has nothing to do with business. It is my life," he said.

His *life*. She was his life. The business was no longer his life. He didn't care what happened with the product launch. It would be successful even if he went out into the street and stole an ice cream cone from a child. It might not be as successful, it might not be as popular, but it didn't functionally matter. Not truly. Yes, he could do more. The company could be bigger. It always could be. It could be more essential. That had been his plan, it had been his legacy, and what was it now? It was hollow. It felt like nothing. It meant nothing.

Verity...

She was everything. She meant everything.

You could wish on that star...

The way she looked at him, with all that hope. But if it were that simple, if he could just wish on a star and have everything be fixed, then he would. He would.

She said that even if it was hard it was worth it...

But there was hard, and there was impossible. And he couldn't...

He thought about the birthday party again. About the way she had seen it. The way that she described him.

He thought about Christmas. Christmas didn't mean anything.

He had an image of a tree, and a house that wasn't his, children opening presents. None for him. For the real family members. A family that he would never be a part of. On the outside looking in.

Christmas didn't mean anything.

Except it did. It had been taken away from him. He had hoped that someone would adopt him and every time they came to see him, he had something taken from him. His hope. With each passing day. He had only been a small boy. He had asked for none of it. None of it. He had only been a boy. He had not been born with a mother who cared for him, but he had been born with hope.

And slowly, very slowly, the world had taken it from him. So he'd had to stop hoping. He had to stop caring. He had to stop believing that he might find someone to care for him. He had given the control over to himself. He had turned it into a choice.

He had built up a wall inside of him so thick and tall and strong that he was the one keeping others out. Instead of the other way around.

He thought of Verity, decorating that ridiculous cake. Her scrawl of Happy Birthday written across the top. No one had ever baked him a birthday cake before. No one had ever told him they loved him.

The president of the board of directors was still talking; he couldn't hear him. He hung up the phone. It rang instantly. He didn't answer it. He didn't care.

Because it was like everything inside of him was falling to pieces. That wall cracking down the middle. "It matters," he said. "It matters."

He saw her. Looking at him across the desk, eating her salad and laughing at him. Talking to him about her day, every detail, great and small. Her, naked in the over-water villa. The way she had been hurt after the encounter with her parents. Her cooking for him, laughing with him. And finally, the museum.

Verity, naked beneath him. He had been certain the

sex with her was some sort of strange magic, conjuring up a feeling that only existed then.

But it was the only place where he lost himself just enough to feel it.

It was the truth. Everything else was a lie.

He had to find her. He had to find her and give her everything.

He closed his eyes, a feeling so big it nearly knocked him over expanding in his chest.

Hope.

CHAPTER SEVENTEEN

VERITY DECIDED THAT she had to stop moping, and go eat at a café or something. Which was how she found herself wandering down the sidewalk feeling sad at 11:00 a.m. in Paris.

"Verity." She stopped, and straightened, goose bumps rising up on her arms. "Cricket."

She turned around, and there was Alex. Well, a version of Alex anyway. This man was not smooth or fathomless. His eyes were not dark voids.

He was on fire.

He ran to her, like he wasn't in public, like there weren't people standing there staring at him. This man could never be confused for a robot. Could never be mistaken for AI. But then, she never had. She had always known.

Yes. She had always known.

"Alex," she said.

"You were right," he said, his voice fractured.

He cupped her face with his hands and leaned down and kissed her. "My beautiful Cricket, you were right. You knew. All this time. That I could feel something.

That I was hiding. I…am so incredibly wounded by the things that happened to me. I don't want that to be true. I want to believe that I'm stronger than that. But I can outrun it. With money, with power. I wanted to believe that I could make a name for myself with this business and have it be the only thing that truly mattered." He took a shuddering breath, his voice shattered. "Money doesn't fix this. And neither does protecting yourself. It only puts a wall in front of all that pain. But it doesn't make it go away. You…you made me knock it down. Because I would rather be in pain. I would rather bleed out on the street and have you for those last moments of my life than live forever safe without you," he whispered. "I did care about Christmas. I did care about my birthday. I wanted those people to adopt me. I wanted my life to be better. I wanted someone to love me. It took thirty-four years. Finally you did. I didn't know what to do with it."

"Of course," she said, holding him close, tears falling already. "Of course."

"I tried to pretend that I was the one in control. That I was the one who didn't care."

"It was never a problem with you, Alex. It was always a flaw in the world, and I know it's hard to believe that. But you always mattered. Always. It isn't your success that makes that true. It's you."

He lowered his head. "When we were in the museum I panicked. I saw myself in the statue, hard and cold. In that painting, foggy and misty and unreachable. And I couldn't bring myself to wish on a star. Because wishing is hope. And I cut myself off from it so long ago. But I need it. I need it or I might as well not even be here. I didn't realize how important it was. I didn't realize what I was missing. Until you walked into my life, and by some miracle, you reached over the wall. You infiltrated. Reached parts of me that no one and nothing ever has. I couldn't even reach."

She touched his face, tilted it upward so his gaze met hers. "You did the same for me. Alex, you did. You really showed me who I am, and what I want. And you made me feel strong enough to ask for it. Demand it, even, even though it hurt."

"I'm so sorry," he said. "My perfect girl. I will never hurt you like that again. I want us to be together. I told the president of the board that I didn't care about the product launch. I don't. I'll tell the whole story, the real story to the whole world."

"You don't have to do that," she said. "I don't need you to prove anything. You're here. And that's proof enough."

"I love you," he said. "I've never said those words to another person. To anything. I love you, Verity."

She closed her eyes, and let them wash over her. "I know," she said. "I'm really glad you said it. But I know, because even if you didn't know it, you were showing me that you loved me. Until you freaked out."

"I'm sorry."

"It had to happen. Just like I had to yell at you after the wedding. Sometimes I think…you have to feel these things. You can't push them down. Not forever. We're going to have to feel difficult things sometimes. But we have each other."

"Yes," he said. "And we…we are a family."

"Yes, Alex," she said, tears filling her eyes. "We are."

He took her hand, and looked down at her. "Where were you headed?"

"To get some lunch."

"I have missed having lunch with you," he said.

"Me too. Salad?"

He threw his head back and laughed, and pulled her into his arms and kissed her. "On second thought. Why don't we skip to dessert."

EPILOGUE

ONE THING ALEX learned over the next decade was that love was an infinitely renewable resource. The love he had for Verity increased by the day, and when she got pregnant with their first child, he felt that love grow. Expand. Change shape as he appreciated new things about her.

When she gave birth to their first child, it was like discovering love all over again.

And the same was true with their second, and their third.

Back at the over-water villa for their anniversary, he had to admit that it was different now. Not so much a grotto of sex and privacy. His children's screams filled the air as they splashed each other in the waves beneath the full moon, the sky scattered with stars.

He gave thanks for the additional rooms they'd had built on a few years back.

"Not exactly a private island anymore," Verity said, sitting beside him, mirroring his thoughts.

"No. It's a family island." He turned to her and smiled. "I think that's better. I've had enough isolation."

"I agree." She grabbed his arm and rested her head on his shoulder. "Look. The stars are out. You could make a wish."

"Little Cricket," he said, kissing her on the head. "Don't you know I already have everything I could ever want?"

* * * * *

If you just couldn't get enough of
Promoted to Boss's Wife,
*then be sure to check out
these other passion-fuelled stories
by Millie Adams!*

Italian's Christmas Acquisition
Billionaire's Bride Bargain
His Highness's Diamond Decree
After-Hours Heir
Dragos's Broken Vows

Available now!